Knights' Quest

A. L. Williams

www.kingdomofnorthumbria.co.uk

All Rights Reserved. No part of this publication may be reproduced, stored in a retrieval system or transmitted in any form or by any means without permission in writing from the publisher.

First published 2006
by AC Group, Stannington, Northumberland, NE61 6DS

Copyright © A.L. Williams

The right of A.L. Williams to be identified as the author of this book has been asserted in accordance with the Copyright, Designs and Patents Act 1988.

ISBN-13: 978-0-9551720-1-4
ISBN-10: 0-9551720-1-2

Designed and produced by AC Group, this book has been typeset in 10/13 pt Century Schoolbook. This publication has been printed and bound in the UK by Cambridge University Press. Special orders and quantities of this book are available for corporations, professional and commercial organisations. For details, telephone AC Group +44 (0)1670 789 489, fax +44 (0)1670 789 464, or e-mail info@ac-group.co.uk.

G   R   O   U   P

Acknowledgements

With special thanks for help with research to: Judith Robinson and her grandson, Tristen; my nephew, Alex Best; Lesley Parr; the Lester family; Sally Eldridge; Andrea Wilson; Ewan Ferguson and Donald H Williams. Proof reading assistance by Susan and Darrell Whittle. The fine illustrations are by Northumbria's specialist book illustrator Sylvia Lynch.

The extract from 'St George and the Dragon' is taken from Thomas Percy's 'Reliques of Ancient English Poetry' (1765).

'The Lambton Worm' was written by C.M. Leumane, and first performed in pantomime at the Tyne Theatre in 1867.

Finally, a big thank-you to my brother Donald Henry, without whose inspiration and encouragement this book would not have been written.

ESPERANCE EN DIEU

Knights' Quest

Harry

A. L. Williams

But the worm got fat an' growed an' growed,
An' growed an aaful size;
He'd greet big teeth, a greet big gob,
An' greet big goggle eyes.
An' when at neets he craaled aboot
To pick up bits o'news,
If he felt dry upon the road,
He milked a dozen coos.

>Whisht! lads, haad yor gobs,
>Aa'll tell ye aall an aaful story,
>Whisht! lads, haad yor gobs,
>An' Aall tell ye 'boot the worm.

This fearful worm wad often feed
On calves an' lambs an' sheep,
An' swally little bairns alive
When they laid doon to sleep.
An' when he'd eaten aall he cud
An' he had had he's fill,
He craaled away an' lapped his tail
Seven times roond Pensher Hill.

from The Lambton Worm
by C.M. Leumane

Thomas

CHAPTER ONE

Harry rides out

It was several hours before Thomas understood the true significance of what he had seen. He wasn't really sure of what he would have done if he had known then. He certainly wasn't about to tell anyone now. The others would just think he was mad, or he had made it up, or both. He wasn't going to give them another excuse to make fun of him.

The boy had just seemed so real. His horse, his old fashioned clothes and his strangely absorbed and exultant look had seemed entirely natural in that setting. If anything, it was Thomas's classmates who seemed out of place, laughing and chatting in small groups of friends as they headed towards the Knights' Yard.

Thinking back, even the castle itself had seemed suddenly different: the ground had been muddier and the whole place even smelt different. Then instantly, just as suddenly, it changed.

One second Thomas had stepped back as the horse with its rider trotted noisily towards him. Another second later, the boy spurred his horse into a gallop. Thomas turned to watch them speed away from the castle. He looked round to see where the rest of the class was. When he glanced back in the direction the horse and rider had taken, they had gone. Where? How? Thomas felt a shiver go down his spine.

He rejoined the others, who were standing next to a statue of a knight on horseback.

'Keep up, Thomas!' called his teacher, Miss Fairfax.

'This is a statue of Harry Hotspur, one of the most famous knights who ever lived. Harry was born here, at Alnwick Castle, in 1364.'

As Miss Fairfax explained how Harry's real name was Sir Henry Percy and that he was the son of the Earl of Northumberland, Thomas thought again about the boy. He was an expert horseman, for sure.

'... Seige of Berwick, where Harry, aged 12, had been given the honour of leading the storming of the castle. He led the charge, brandishing his sword and shouting the Percy motto, *"Esperance!"*'

Thomas thought back to the moment when he looked back and had discovered the boy and his horse had disappeared from sight. How was this possible? When he had looked over his shoulder again, he couldn't see anywhere that they could have disappeared from view.

Miss Fairfax continued: 'The Scots gave him the nickname 'Harry Hotspur' because of his skill and speed in battle. Harry was brave, but he was also hot-headed. When the Scots were returning from raiding Northumberland, Harry and his followers attacked, instead of waiting for the forces of the Prince Bishop of Durham to join them. Although the Scottish leader, Earl Douglas, was killed at the battle of Otterburn, the English were defeated. Harry was captured and a ransom had to be paid for his release.'

Thomas sighed. Maybe he had just imagined it. There was nowhere the horse and rider could have gone in that short space of time. What was more, no one else seemed to have taken the slightest notice of the lad on the horse.

Miss Fairfax finished talking. She looked around to make sure that she could see where all the children from her class were. The way she turned her head reminded Thomas of a hawk he had seen at a falconry display. She was intensely aware of what was going on around her. Tall and angular, Miss Fairfax had short red hair, piercing blue eyes and freckles. There was no possibility of any of her class wandering off, Miss Fairfax was one of those teachers who knew exactly what was what and who was where.

Some of the girls took photos of each other next to the statue. The knight on the statue was in a heroic pose, wearing full armour, carrying a lance and his horse was rearing up impressively.

The rest of the class went into the Knights' Yard. Thomas followed, feeling a bit left out. He had started at his new school that week. The trip to Alnwick Castle had sounded fun, though Thomas had still felt nervous about going because he hadn't made any friends at the school yet.

When he had boarded the coach that morning everyone was sitting with friends. Thomas was going to sit by himself, but Miss Fairfax insisted that he sat next to her. Thomas just knew the boys at the back were laughing at him and calling him a teacher's pet. He could hear one of them mimicking Miss Fairfax and saying, 'Thomas! Come and sit here.' Miss Fairfax was talking to the driver at the time or the boy wouldn't have dared. Thomas shot a look at the boy. He had short blond hair and a cheeky grin. He saw Thomas looking at him and laughed even more.

During the journey Miss Fairfax explained to Thomas what they were going to do when they arrived at the castle. They were going to the Knights' Yard, where lots of different activities had been laid on for them. They were going to dress up as knights and ladies and imagine they had been transported back in time seven hundred years. They were joining the Knights' School to find out how pages became squires and how squires became knights.

'Would you like to go back seven hundred years and meet one of the fourteenth century knights from that time, Thomas?' asked Miss Fairfax.

Thomas always had a careful approach to life (this was partially in response to his parents, who seemed to him to be completely crazy), so he said, 'I'd much rather stay in the twenty-first century and meet the fourteenth century knight today.'

Thomas usually had a thoughtful expression on his face. He did not often say what he was thinking, as he was quite shy. He looked out of the window at the distant view of the castle. The castle was everything a castle should be – there were battlements, towers, and a gatehouse. The castle was massive and dominated the landscape. His blue eyes shone with excitement at the thought of visiting it.

Like the other children, he was wearing school uniform. Thomas's blue jumper with the St Wilfrid's badge was brand new. His brown hair was neatly styled, as his mother had insisted that he had his hair cut before he started at his new school. She had said he looked really smart when he set off for school that morning.

Now Thomas was finally in the Knights' Yard and about to find out what he was going to do. The class had gathered around Miss Fairfax at one of the information boards. It seemed they were going to follow in the footsteps of a young boy named Thomas on his journey from starting as a page to becoming a knight. Thomas groaned inwardly when he heard the character's name. He just knew one of the lads would make some kind of stupid comment on it being the same as his.

It didn't take long.

Thomas was hanging back from the main group and Miss

Fairfax called, 'Come along now, Thomas!'

Thomas heard the one of boys snigger and say, 'Thomas is going to be Miss Fairfax's page.' It was the blond boy with the short hair again. Thomas cast him a filthy look and went to catch up with Miss Fairfax before she called out again.

The class moved straight to the dressing up. Once they were fully kitted out, they were going try out all the different activities. One of the girls, Maya Patel, wanted to dress up as a knight because she was very keen to do some sword fighting. Miss Fairfax said she could.

One of the staff from the castle was going to demonstrate. He was dressed like a knight and showed them the basics of fighting with a longsword. In training, the pages would have practised with wooden swords. The children were given plastic ones.

They were going to practise in pairs. Of course, Thomas did not have a partner. Neither did Maya. Her friends had gone off to the castle building activity. Maya asked Thomas if he would like to sword fight. Thomas said, 'Yes,' rather half-heartedly, as he didn't really want to fight with a girl.

The knight's costume had a sort of balaclava helmet. Maya's short, shoulder length hair framed her face. She had a lively expression and seemed determined to enjoy herself.

Maya was actually very good at sword fighting. She was very quick, very agile and could spot an opening before Thomas realised it was there. The Alnwick Castle knight said she was really talented and in the end, Thomas was glad he was fighting her. When they had to move on to the next activity, Thomas thanked her and she smiled back.

Thomas looked round the yard. In the centre was a pavilion, a striped circular knight's tent. There was a covered paved area around the perimeter of the yard where most of the activities were. There was no sign of the boy, or his horse.

Thomas still could not get that boy on horseback out of his

head. He thought he would ask one of the costumed Castle helpers.

'Is there a boy here who dresses up in fourteenth century clothes and rides around on a horse?'

The Castle lady smiled. She shook her head and the piece of fabric attached to her medieval hat waved in the breeze.

'No, we don't have any boys on horses here today.'

That was it then. He had imagined the boy. There could not be any other explanation.

After skittles, castle building and coat of arms designing, Thomas made his way to the jousting. While he was listening to the explanation of what this involved, Thomas spotted the boy, who was watching the re-enactment intently. His horse was nowhere to be seen.

The boy looked a couple of years older than Thomas, maybe twelve or thirteen. He was tall and thin, with blond hair. His clothes were what you would expect for a nobleman from the fourteenth century: doublet and hose in fine blue wool and neatly made brown leather boots, fitted with silver spurs.

Thomas stared at the boy, wondering if he would do his vanishing trick again. There was no way he was going to take his eyes off him even for a second.

The boy looked up directly at Thomas, smiled, winked … and disappeared!

CHAPTER TWO

Be careful what you wish for

Next day was a school day. Thomas was one of the first to line up to go into the classroom. The other boys had been playing football in the yard. He felt left out and had spent the five minutes before school started just hanging around hoping some one would speak to him. 'If only I were back at my old school, with my old friends,' he thought.

Miss Fairfax let them in and took the register. Thomas still didn't know all the names of the others in his class. He sat on the same table as Maya, who smiled at him. He felt a bit better for this.

Miss Faifax explained what they were going to be doing that day. English to start with… more on the Lambton Worm and knights.

On the display board she had put up the huge poster of the vivid green worm that they had made to illustrate the story.

They began by listening to a recording of the song and

then singing it themselves. Thomas liked singing the chorus. He normally got told off if he said 'Shut yor gob!'

Everyone else seemed to like singing it too:

> *Whisht! lads, haad yor gobs,*
> *Aa'll tell yer aall an aaful story,*
> *Whisht! lads, haad yor gobs*
> *An' aa'll tell ye aboot the worm.*

By the time they got to the last chorus they were very loud indeed. Especially when they sang 'gobs'!

They were a bit noisy afterwards and Miss Fairfax said now she was going to have to ask them to 'Haad yor gobs', which made everybody laugh again.

Then Miss Fairfax asked, 'What things have we found out about the worm?'

Each group had two minutes to see who could find the most things. The children on Thomas' table started their list. Maya wrote it down.

1. *It was a sort of dragon.*
2. *With big teeth*
3. *Big gob*
4. *Goggley eyes*
5. *It came from the River Wear*
6. *It lived in the well where Sir John had thrown it*
7. *It grew bigger and fatter*
8. *It swallowed children*
9. *And sheep*
10. *It liked to eat lambs*
11. *And eat calves too*
12. *It drinks milk*
13. *It can milk cows*
14. *Sir John killed it by cutting it into three 'halves'*

Thomas wanted to say something, but everyone had got in

with what he wanted to say before he had had a chance to say it. His table had the same number of things as the next table.

Maya said, 'Sir John caught it on a hook.' They had fifteen now.

Miss Fairfax asked how many each group had got. Another group had fifteen. Thomas then thought of another one, but he didn't want to say it to the whole class, so he whispered it to Maya. 'It curled itself around Penshaw Hill seven times.'

'Miss, we've thought of another one!' Maya said. His table had won and everyone round it smiled at him now. Thomas was starting to feel things were getting better and his new school might not be so bad.

Later, after reading time, Miss Fairfax told them about an older version of the story. In this story the worm was completely black, with the head of a salamander (a sort of lizard) with needle sharp teeth. It left a trail of black slime. The wise woman of Brugeford advised John Lambton to fight the worm wearing armour studded with double-edged spikes. When the worm had coiled round him and tried to crush him, it tore itself to shreds. Thomas thought the worm sounded a bit like a python in the way it attacked its victims. There was a curse in this story. John Lambton had to kill the first thing that crossed his path as he crossed the threshold of Lambton Hall. If he didn't, then 'three times three generations of Lambtons would not die in their beds.' John had thought to get round this by having his servant release his dog when he made a pre-arranged signal (three blasts on his horn). He would kill the dog when he crossed the threshold. Unfortunately, the servant didn't release the dog before John's father met him. Obviously he didn't kill his own father: his plan had been to kill his dog. The family was cursed.

It struck Thomas that dragon killing was far more complicated than he had previously thought. It wasn't simply the case knights went after them with sharp swords and nice shiny suits of armour. The whole business has to be carefully considered, including possible side curses and special equipment.

He was just wondering how other dragons might have been killed or otherwise got rid of, when Miss Fairfax briskly announced it was time to go to the hall for the school assembly.

Thomas soon changed his mind about school not being so bad.

Some of the boys from his class deliberately pushed him when they were in the corridor. When they got to the hall, the boys hadn't left a space for him to sit. Maya got the girls to budge up, so he sat down next to her and on the end of the boys' section. He heard the boys whispering his name and Maya's and nudging each other and he felt sure his face had turned red with embarrassment. It didn't seem to bother Maya though.

Thomas made himself think about something else. It was P.E. next. It would be cricket. Great. Thomas loved cricket and had been on the school team at his last school. Bowling was what he enjoyed best.

After the assembly, which was about how it was important to be kind and considerate to others, the class went to get changed. One of the boys picked up one of Thomas's trainers and threw it to the other side of the room. Another kicked it under the bench. It became a game to try and stop Thomas getting his trainer. Steve, who was one of the boys who sat on the same table in class as Thomas, did not try to stop them, but he did not join in either. He seemed to be in a world of his own. By the time Thomas had retrieved his trainer and had got changed, he was the last to run out onto the field, just after Steve.

Miss Fairfax got them to warm up and they played some throwing and catching games, then it was time to pick sides. Steve Armstrong and Jenny Graham were picking their teams. Thomas knew Steve wouldn't pick him. He had never even spoken to Jenny. He wasn't surprised to be the last picked. It was the first time this had ever happened to him and he hated it. Steve went into bat first, having won the toss. On the pitch, Steve looked completely different. Alert and relaxed, he looked towards the bowler. He was quite a good batsman and Thomas longed for the chance to bowl against him. However, the only time Thomas actually handled the ball was when Steve sent a long low ball in his direction. He fielded it efficiently and that was it.

The lesson was over before he had had a chance to bat and, of course, he didn't get to bowl. He was actually glad when it was time to go in to do some Maths.

Thomas usually found Maths easy. He finished quickly while everyone was still working. He pretended he hadn't because he did not want to stand out. To pass the time he started thinking about dragons. They seemed to present real challenges to the knights who fought them. 'I wish I had a chance to fight a dragon,' he thought. Immediately he almost heard his mother's voice saying, 'Be careful what you wish for, Thomas. You might just get it.' At the same time, out of the corner of his eye he noticed something moving on the field. It was the boy and his horse. The boy waved at him! Thomas was so surprised that he dropped his pencil. It clattered to the floor. He looked round. No one else seemed to have noticed the boy. Miss Fairfax was looking at him. He bent down to pick his pencil up and then looked out of the window again. The boy was gone. 'I must be dreaming,' he thought. He was certain that if the others had seen anything, they would all be pointing and staring out of the windows by now.

To his horror, Miss Fairfax had realised he had finished and, after looking at his work, which was perfectly correct, said he would be doing a Maths challenge next Maths lesson. He knew everyone was looking at him and was certain his face had gone bright red again. He was too embarrassed to ask what a Maths challenge was.

The day dragged on. Lunchtime (with no one to play with) was the worst. A well-meaning midday supervisor persuaded a group of older boys to let him join in with their game of football. They wouldn't pass the ball to him and soon as he got the ball they kicked him, so he dropped out as soon as he felt he could. He lurked around the door to the hall, waiting for his class to go in for lunch. After what seemed ages, the dinner lady called Miss Fairfax's class into lunch.

As he queued he heard one of the dinner ladies talking.

'Did you hear that James Armstrong was arrested for the fight at the pub?' He remembered that the fight had been on the news and his mum had commented that the pub concerned, the Blue Lion, was only round the corner from them. She was shocked that anything like this could happen in this village. There had been about ten people involved and someone had been knifed.

Thomas wondered if James was related to Steve. He didn't have long to wait as he overheard some of the other boys talking about Steve's brother being arrested. Thomas heard a row break out in the queue behind him. Steve seemed to be having an argument with someone. He kept shouting, 'He didn't do it! He didn't do it!' The dinner ladies rushed over to separate them and took both boys out of the hall.

Steve wasn't in the classroom after lunch. He rejoined the class after quiet reading time, just in time for the science lesson. Miss Fairfax gave the whole class one of those looks, so no one dared ask him where he had been. Steve still looked very angry, so no one would have asked anyway. His face was red. He stood in the doorway for a moment, then stalked over to his seat and sat down quickly. He ran his hand through his short blond hair and stared at the desk, not looking at anyone sat at the table.

They had a worksheet on energy to do, which had lots of

sentences to complete. It took Thomas all of his energy to stay awake, as the worksheet was so boring. He started thinking about dragons again. Some dragons were said to breathe fire. Where did the fire come from? Was it really just the dragon's breath? How did the dragons get it to catch fire? Was the breath a bit like rocket fuel?

Home time! At last! Thomas could not wait to go home. He rushed outside. A group of boys were standing outside. Steve came out to join them. Because of all the noise around him, Thomas couldn't hear what they said, but he got the impression there might be some trouble from the way they jostled round Steve.

He didn't wait to find out what it was. Steve was not his friend. He ran all the way home.

Steve

CHAPTER THREE

An Imaginary Friend?

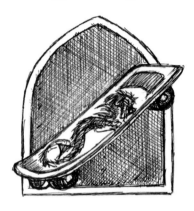

'Saturday. No school. Brilliant! Yes!'

Those were Thomas's first thoughts as he stretched himself, then leapt out of bed. 'My new skateboard!' was his next thought. He had bought it earlier in the week with his birthday money. He hadn't had a chance to customise it yet. His had a red deck and he thought he might make a flame design on it, like dragon's breath.

The nearest skate park was in Amble. Maybe his dad would take him one Saturday when he didn't have a cricket match. The local park would be fine for today.

He wanted to practise his jumps and there was a place that he thought would be good for 'ollies'.

Thomas grabbed some breakfast, told his Mum where he was going, fastened his helmet and set off. He was about halfway down the street when he saw Steve. Steve was with an older boy, helping him with his paper round. Thomas guessed it was one of his brothers. They both had BMX bikes.

He said 'Hello' as he passed. Steven looked at him as if he was seeing him for the first time. 'Hi,' he said, stuffing a paper through a letterbox.

The park was empty, as it was still early. Ideal. Thomas practised. First the crouch, then stretch up, pressing down on the rear foot, then slide front foot forward, switching the pressure forwards, lifting up the rear foot … take off! Ok, it was only a beginner's trick, he thought. But it felt so good to do a really perfect jump.

He had just got the landing absolutely spot-on, when he noticed the boy from the castle was there. He was standing nearby. Thomas had the distinct impression he might have been watching for a while.

'You're Harry Hotspur, aren't you?' Thomas asked. He wasn't sure how he knew, he just did. Maybe it was the boy's shiny spurs that had given him the idea.

Harry laughed. 'Aye, that's what folk caall me. Who are ye?'

'Thomas Malton.'

Noticing how fascinated Harry was with the board, Thomas said, gesturing towards it, 'Would you like a go?' Harry most definitely would. He declined the offer of the helmet, laughing and saying he wouldn't need it. 'Ah'm a ghost, after aal!'

Thomas thought, 'He admits he's a ghost!' Then, 'Well, at least he knows he is a ghost.' He didn't know why he found this very reassuring. Maybe it was the matter of fact way Harry had said it, as if it didn't matter. Harry had an old fashioned way of speaking. He had the Northumbrian accent though, like most of Thomas's old friends, so it seemed entirely natural to be taking it in turns to do ollies and try doing nollies with him.

It was a new experience for Thomas to be demonstrating how to do skateboarding tricks. He had always been the one who had been doing the learning. His old friend Robbie had been the first to have a skateboard and had taught Thomas the basics.

Time passed really quickly. For the first time since he had moved here from Hexham, Thomas was having fun with a friend. He didn't care whether his friend was real or imaginary. Or for that matter, if he had been real and was now imaginary.

Harry was a fast learner and had great balance. He was absolutely fearless. Thomas supposed that Harry would not feel any pain if he fell off. Just the same, Thomas knew that this fearlessness was just part of Harry, whether he was alive or whether he was a ghost.

Thomas did not notice them straight away. Harry stopped skateboarding though, the moment they came into view.

It was the same group of boys who had been waiting for Steve yesterday. One of them was kicking a football along. The others were laughing about something. Then they spotted him and one of them made some comment. They didn't seem to notice Harry. They would surely have had more to say to each other if they had. Harry watched them steadily.

Thomas felt uneasy. He did not know if they would bother him. However, there was only one way out of the park and that was in their direction.

When they approached, he knew, from the way they laughed and nudged each other, that trouble was coming.

Harry glanced sideways at Thomas and then positioned himself just in front of him and slightly to his left.

'Gizza go on yor board then!' said the boy in the middle, staring at Thomas.

'Nah,' said Thomas, poised for flight.

Two of them lunged towards him. They obviously couldn't see Harry, who somehow managed to trip them up. As they went sprawling, Thomas heard Harry shout 'Go!'

Thomas leapt on his board and shot down the banking

path faster than he had ever done before, twisting with each turn of the path. His heart was thumping.

He heard the boys shouting after him. He didn't look back. He could hear footsteps starting to follow him down the hill.

At the park gates he saw Maya. 'Thomas,' she called, 'Are you all right? Are those boys after you?'

'Yes,' he said, barely able to catch his breath.

'Follow me,' Maya said. Thomas felt he could trust Maya, so he did. She ran quickly round the corner into Dalbeattie Crescent, then darted up the garden path of the first house. 'Come on!' Maya opened the front door. They shut the front door. Thomas drew a long breath. Maya went to the window and looked out. The boys had run round the corner. They stood talking in front of the house for a few moments. One of them shrugged his shoulders and then headed back towards the park. Then the rest turned back too.

'They've gone.'

'They'll think we have disappeared,' said Thomas, heaving a huge sigh of relief.

'Yes,' said Maya, looking curiously at Thomas. 'A bit like the strange boy you were with did. Who was he?'

Thomas realised Maya had seen Harry. How was he going to explain to her who Harry was? Would she believe him if he did?

CHAPTER FOUR

A real friend

'Hello,' said Maya's mum.

'Saved!' thought Thomas. He wouldn't need to answer Maya's question now.

'This is Thomas, Mum. He has just started at my school,' said Maya. Her mum smiled at Thomas and asked him if he would like something to drink.

A small tabby cat with a white face and white paws came up to Thomas. 'That's my cat, Smokey,' said Maya.

Smokey followed them into the kitchen, purring.

Thomas sat at the pine kitchen table, with a glass of orange juice and biscuits, chatting to Maya and her mum about skateboarding and the school trip to Alnwick Castle.

Maya had a new computer game, 'Knights' Quest', and asked Thomas if he'd like to have a go. The computer was in a corner of the lounge, next to a bookcase with a gleaming row of sports trophies on the top.

Maya explained what you had to do. Basically you chose a knight who had to fight different opponents, mainly strange creatures such as dragons. After Thomas's knight had killed a few creatures and had been killed a few times himself, Maya repeated her question, 'Who was the boy you were with?'

Thomas thought for a moment. 'What exactly did you see?' he asked cautiously.

'From where I was standing, it looked as if that boy tripped up two of the boys who were after you,' she said. 'The strange thing was they didn't seem to notice him. Why was he wearing those old fashioned clothes? Why did he bow to me? How did he disappear?'

'Well, I am not sure if you are going to believe this, Maya. The boy is Harry Hotspur, which is why he was wearing the medieval clothes. He is a ghost. Not everyone can see him, which is why he was able somehow to trip the boys up. He must have realised you could see him, though, which is why he bowed to you.'

Thomas looked at her. He was not in the least sure how she would react.

'I suppose that explains how he was able to vanish the way he did,' said Maya thoughtfully.

'Please don't mention this to anyone else, Maya. Most people wouldn't believe you.'

Maya agreed not to say anything to anybody.

Thomas explained how he had seen Harry at Alnwick and on the school field, as well as on the park, where they had skateboarded.

'He seems to be haunting you!' said Maya. 'I wonder why?'

Thomas hadn't thought of it in that way. Was he being haunted? If so, as Maya said, why?

Just then Mrs Patel put her head round the door. 'You have another visitor. Maya. It's Steven from next door.'

Steve came in. When he saw Thomas, he grinned and said, 'Hi! I guessed you were here when I saw the skateboard in the hall.'

'Thomas had some trouble from Alan Milton and his mates,' said Maya.

'They wanted to take my board,' said Thomas.

'Who was with them?' asked Steve.

'I don't know their names. One was tall, with black hair.'

'That's Martin Glendinning,' said Maya.

'Then there was one with brown hair and glasses.'

'That's David Scott.'

'There was someone wearing a Newcastle United shirt. He had red hair and freckles.'

'That's Alan.'

It had been Alan who had asked him for a go on his board. Thomas hadn't liked the way he'd asked and he had felt he might not get his board back. Judging from the way Alan and David had tried to grab it, he felt certain that was likely.

'I had some trouble from them yesterday, too. They were hanging around waiting for me after school,' said Steve.

Thomas was embarrassed. He felt guilty for not having stayed to make sure Steve was ok. At the time, he had just thought to himself that Steve wasn't a friend of his, so it wasn't his business.

'What happened?'

'Alan is after me because he thinks my brother was the one who knifed his brother, Terry. He wants to fight me, just because James is my brother. He and his mates had just got their hands on me when Miss Fairfax saw what was going on. She took Alan and the others to see Mr Montgomery.'

'Who is Mr Montgomery?'

'He is our head teacher and he is very strict. I wouldn't have liked to be in their shoes.'

Maya's mum came into the room. 'Steve and Maya, we will need to set off for Judo in about five minutes.'

'Judo?'

Looking at the bookcase, Thomas realised that Maya's

name was engraved on the trophies. She must be really good at Judo.

Maya's mum saw him and laughed. 'Yes. They are all Maya's.'

'Mum!' It was Maya's turn to be embarrassed.

'Five minutes and then we have to go.'

After Maya's mum had gone back to the kitchen, Steve explained that his brother had gone to the Blue Lion for a darts match. Most of the people in the bar were watching the final game, when glancing out of the window, James saw a fight start in the car park. Most of the lads fighting were people he'd been to school with. James thought he could reason with them and stop the fight. They didn't listen. They had been drinking.

Then Terry took out a knife. James had tried to take it from him. 'He knows he was stupid to try,' said Steve. 'He grabbed Terry's hand and tried to wrestle the knife out of it. Then Terry slipped. His wrist was cut accidentally. There was blood everywhere. James said the others stopped fighting. They all stared at Terry. Some people came out of the pub. The others ran off. James gave Terry first aid. He had made him lie down and hold his hand up, holding the cut to try to slow the bleeding. Terry had had to go to hospital, as he needed stitches. James went inside with the landlord. When the police arrived they found the knife with James' fingerprints on it.' Steve sighed. 'James has been arrested. The others are letting him take the blame. It isn't fair.'

'What about Terry?' said Maya. 'Do you think he will speak up for James?'

'I don't know.' Steve didn't look hopeful. 'Maybe. Or maybe he won't want to admit it was his knife, so he won't get into trouble with the police.'

CHAPTER FIVE

Safety in Numbers

It was Monday. 'Time to get up, Thomas!' called his mum. 'School. Oh no!' Thomas winced at the thought. He could not believe it. The weekend had gone too quickly. He got ready slowly. He was dreading school.

Just before Thomas was due to set off, there was a knock at the door. 'It's two of your friends for you,' said his mum, looking through the window. Thomas bounded to the door. It was Maya and Steve.

'Hello,' he said. Then picked up his bag and headed for the door.

'Aren't you going to say goodbye?' said his mum, smiling.

'Bye,' he said awkwardly. He usually gave her a hug before he left. At least he had since he started at this new school. He didn't want his friends to see him hugging his mum, though. He rushed out of the door, paused, looked at his mum and waved goodbye before he shut the door.

'Thanks for calling for me,' he said when had joined the others.

'That's ok', said Maya. 'We thought there might be safety

in numbers. Alan and his gang seem to have it in for you and Steve.'

As they walked past the newsagents. Thomas spotted the headline on the board outside: 'Big Dig at Wormhill'.

'What's that about?'

'I had a look at a paper on the round this morning. It's the University archaeology team – they're going to dig up Wormhill. They think it might be where a Saxon chief is buried.' Steve looked thoughtful.

'I wonder if it will disturb the dragon,' said Maya.

'What dragon?'

'There is supposed to be a dragon under the hill, guarding the chief and his treasure. Anyone who disturbs it will bring a curse on the land, unless the dragon is defeated.'

'That's why the hill is called Wormhill. It's because of the worm,' said Steve.

'Do the archaeologists know about the curse?' asked Thomas.

'They are sure to,' said Steve. 'They probably just think it is a story.'

They turned round the corner and could see St Wilfrid's First School ahead.

'Uh-oh,' said Steve.

There was a small group of boys hanging around the gates. Thomas recognised the boys from the park. He felt his shoulders tighten and he gripped his bag tightly.

Steve's jaw set. Only Maya seemed nonchalant and continued to walk calmly towards the entrance. She paused at the gates to wait for Steve and Thomas.

The bell rang. It could just be heard above the noise of children playing outside the school. A tall teacher, who was wearing a suit, strode up to the gates.

'Who's that?' asked Thomas. He had half-guessed the answer.

'That's Mr Montgomery,' said Steve.

As soon as they saw him, the group of boys went inside to line up outside their classrooms.

'Hurry along now! The bell has gone!' Mr Montgomery said sternly. He had given the group of boys a funny look after he had seen Steve and Thomas standing back.

'He knows something is going on,' thought Thomas.

Thomas relaxed. He and Steve rejoined Maya outside Miss Fairfax's classroom.

The morning started with Maths. Miss Fairfax had not forgotten Thomas's Maths Challenge. She gave him a pack of work sheets. The first ones were about number patterns, including Fibonacci numbers. This pattern was easy to work out. There were some pictures showing how this pattern occurred in nature. There were pictures of sunflower seed heads, pinecones and plants. There was an explanation of how you could use the Fibonacci sequence to make a spiral. There was also a different sort of spiral and with a different way of working it out, but Thomas did not get as far as the explanation of that one, when it was time for English and back to the Lambton worm.

Almost straight away, someone asked Miss Fairfax about the dig at Wormhill. 'What about the dragon, Miss?'

Thomas listened intently.

Miss Fairfax said, 'Like the Lambton worm, the story is an old one and there maybe some parts of it that are true, but most of it isn't. The story is that there is a dragon underneath Wormhill, guarding the burial site of a dead king. The archaeologists think that this part might have some truth.

'There is a good reason why people think there might be a dragon there and that is the shape of the hill. It has ridges on it, as if a dragon might have coiled itself around it. This might be why the story of the dragon was made up. However good the story is, dragons don't exist and never have.

'We know that Wormhill was important for centuries as a

place of worship, because of the spiral turf maze at the bottom of the hill, near to the spring, which was also thought to be holy.'

'What was the turf maze for?' This was the first question Thomas had asked since he had joined the class. Miss Fairfax looked at him carefully, with a slight smile on her face.

'Well, no one is really certain as to how they were used. They seem to have had religious significance. There are quite a few of these mazes in England, made from grass or stone paths. They have one path that you follow into the centre, not a choice of paths like you have with modern mazes. With the spiral at Wormhill, people have suggested that the worshippers at the maze thought that the journey to the centre represented the journey through life and the journey out was the afterlife.'

'A bit like time-travel,' Thomas thought.

'I'll draw a spiral maze on the board,' said Miss Fairfax, 'You might notice something else which is unusual about this maze. If this was a maze with walls, and you walked into the centre touching one of the walls, would you be able to go out again without touching the same bit of wall?'

It didn't take long for the class to discover that you could go in touching one side of the wall and out touching the other.

Thomas thought he would definitely pay a visit to the maze at Wormhill after school. It wasn't too far from the village.

Lunchtime was great. Thomas played tag with Steve and Maya's friends. The bullies kept their distance. This was because wherever Steve went on the playground, a lunchtime supervisor didn't seem to be too far away.

At home time, Mr Montgomery was by the gates. He let Steve, Maya and Thomas pass, but for some reason had wanted a quiet word with Alan and his mates. Long enough for the three friends to get round the corner and out of sight of the school.

They had agreed to meet up later and show Thomas Wormhill.

Just outside the village, Wormhill lived up to its name. It looked like a giant worm hill. Sure enough, the ridges round it looked exactly as if an enormous dragon had made them. Thomas tried estimating how big the dragon could have been, then gave up when he saw the maze.

It was a flat maze and had originally been made by carving the turf. The villagers had kept up the tradition and it was well maintained. It did make you feel a bit dizzy if you ran round it quickly, which is what they did.

Collapsing in a heap of laughter, Thomas did not hear the shouts at first. It was Alan Milton and his gang. He scrambled to his feet. He noticed Maya had moved in front of him and Steve. He thought that was odd. Then the gang rushed towards them and he didn't have time to think.

Thump! Almost as soon as Alan tried to push Maya out of the way, he seemed to end up flat on his back, sprawled out in front of Thomas. He realised that Maya had thrown Alan. It had happened so fast that everyone, apart from Maya and Steve, seemed bewildered by it.

'What?' said Alan.

Steve laughed. 'Maya is a Judo champion, Alan. I wouldn't try to push her aside again if I were you.'

The rest of the gang had stopped in their tracks and were looking at Maya in a stunned sort of way. 'A bit like a row of goldfishes' was the way Thomas remembered them that evening, when he was persuading his mum to let him join the Judo club.

'Come on,' said Maya, 'Let's go home.' The gang did not try to follow them. They walked away, passing a group of people who were setting up tents and unloading a minibus full of equipment in the field near to the road. The archaeologists had arrived.

Thomas lay awake that night. So much had happened over

the last few days that he found it difficult to go to sleep. His mum and dad always made jokes about counting sheep if you found it hard to go to sleep. It never worked. Maybe more complicated counting might do the trick. Perhaps the Fibonacci sequence might work: 0, 1, 1, 2, 3, 5, 8, 13, 21, 34, 55, 89,144, 233, 377, 610, 987...

Thomas was at Wormhill again. He noticed the spiral ridge that had given the hill its name. Then it was as if he were floating above the hill. On one side of it was the spiral turf maze that was to one side of the spring. He heard himself saying the sequence again. Zero, one... The top of the hill seemed to move! He paused, then said one again. He counted to two, saying two aloud, then to three, saying three aloud with the third count. With each number that he spoke aloud, the hill stirred. First a huge green head uncurled, then a neck started to emerge. Five, eight, thirteen...

As the dragon continued to unwind in a ghastly stop and start sequence, Thomas mentally checked off the list of dragon characteristics: salamander head, big teeth, big gob, and goggley eyes. At thirty-four, the dragon shook itself, yawned and breathed in with a strange rattling and hissing sound, then breathed out a huge blast of fire.

'It's a nightmare,' Thomas thought. 'This is not real. This can't be happening.' Part of him was absolutely convinced that it was real. 'Just as real as Harry Hotspur.'

'How can I stop this?' was his next thought, as the dragon unfurled its huge bat-like wings. 'Maybe if I reverse the sequence...'

Thomas held his breath he reached thirty-four. The dragon furled its wings, yawned and breathed in. Once the dragon had disappeared back into the hillside, Thomas fell into a deep dreamless sleep.

So deep that he did not hear the sound of fire sirens screaming through the village.

CHAPTER SIX

Fire and Water

Dad was still at home when Thomas came downstairs for breakfast next day. He didn't seem at all his usual cheery self. In fact, he didn't seem to notice Thomas coming into the room.

The news was on: 'There has been a major fire at one of the North East's oldest factories, Dainty's. Dainty's Tableware has been manufacturing tablemats and other fancy goods for nearly a century and is still owned by the Dainty family. No one was injured by last night's fire. Passers-by reported that the whole of the roof suddenly caught fire at once. Three fire engines were called to the blaze. The managing Director, Paul Dainty, says that the factory is unlikely to re-open at this site and he will transfer production to the firm's Leeds factory. The union predicts that all fifty jobs could go.'

This was where Thomas's dad worked. No wonder he looked upset.

'Does that mean you will lose your job, Dad?'

'We'll wait and see, Thomas. Lizzie, I am going to see if they have finished damping down the fire and if there is anything I can do.'

'Well, be careful, John. You don't want the roof falling in on you.'

'Not much chance of that. It was the roof which went first and I don't think that there's much of it left.'

'How did it happen?' Thomas asked.

'Well, son, I don't know. No one really knows why. Maybe the Fire Brigade will be able to give us more information. Anyway, the whole roof seemed to catch fire in one go. I spoke to one fireman and he said he'd never seen or heard of anything like it.'

All people talked about that day was the fire. Quite a few people from the village worked at Dainty's and were really worried about their jobs. There was a rush to buy newspapers, which had pictures of the fire and the headline: *'Jobs Go Up In Smoke.'*

Even at school, the children were talking about it. Robbie Fraser's dad was a fireman and a small group of children were standing clustered around him, listening to what Robbie's dad had told him about the blaze.

'He said he hadn't seen anything like it since he was in the army. He didn't think it was possible for the whole roof to go up in flames so fast, without some sort of a gigantic flame-thrower.'

The bell went and the children reluctantly left to line up by the classroom doors.

Thomas wondered about the coincidence of his dream of the fire-breathing dragon. Maybe it was not surprising that he was dreaming about dragons when that's all they seemed to be doing in English. Today Miss Fairfax was telling them the story of another local dragon, the Longwitton dragon. The story was similar in the basics: knight meets dragon, dragon dies. 'Another case of dragonocide,' he thought, 'that is, if there is such a word.' His own piece of writing for English had the title: 'Myth or Monster? A Quest for the Truth about Dragons.'

The title was about the most exciting bit about it. Perhaps dragons were just a load of old ballads. All Thomas really had was a list of questions, the first of which was, 'If dragons never existed, why are there so many stories about them?' It was annoying having all these questions and no answers.

Maths came and went. This time in the Maths Challenge there was a different sort of spiral, an Archimedes spiral. It looked neater somehow. The mathematics of it was interesting. It was possible to work out formulae to explain all of it. That was the great thing about Maths. There was so much that was definable. Miss Fairfax had looked over the work he had done so far. She told him that spirals had fascinated generations of people and they had found some Bronze Age spirals carved into rocks near Alnwick. Like the turf maze, no one really knew why they were there, but it was assumed there was some religious significance to them. Another mystery. Thomas sighed.

Instead of arranging to meet his friends after school, Thomas decided he had better stay at home. He had a feeling that it would be his turn to cheer his dad up. It was usually the other way round. Dad had been great about trying to cheer Thomas up when they had moved here from Hexham. If his dad had lost his job, it would be a great blow. He had been so pleased to get the foreman's job at Dainty's. For the first time, the family had been able to afford to buy their home, instead of renting. Dad had spent every weekend decorating their terrace house.

Anyway, it was time for Operation Cheer Dad Up. When Thomas arrived home though, there was no Dad to be seen. 'He has gone to Leeds,' said his mum. 'He is going to be back at the weekend. They are trying to work out how they are going to fill all the orders the factory had on its books.'

His mum looked sad though, so Thomas thought he'd keep her company and told her some of the latest jokes Steve had told him.

'What's the favourite game of mice?'

'I don't know, ' she said smiling.

'Hide and squeak.' It made her laugh. Thomas helped with the dinner and the washing up, which was something he didn't normally do. The phone rang. It was Dad. His mum told him how helpful Thomas had been and his dad asked to speak to him. 'Well done, Thomas. It's good to know Mum has you to rely on while I'm away. Are you up for a game of cricket on the park when I get back?'

'Sure Dad. If it stops raining that is. It has been tipping it down here today.'

'See you soon, son.'

That night, Thomas had another dream about a dragon. It was the Longwitton dragon story this time. What was different though was Thomas wasn't alone. Harry was watching the story unfold with him. The difference from Miss Fairfax's version was Harry Hotspur's expert commentary on the techniques used by the knight to defeat the dragon.

The setting was the Longwitton woods. There were three wells within the woods that were said to have healing powers and the dream began with a local ploughman going to one of the wells and seeing the dragon lapping up the water with its long black tongue. As soon as it was aware of the ploughman, the dragon disappeared.

The ploughman did not hang about either. When he got back to Longwitton, he told everyone about the dragon and swore that he had known that the dragon was still there by the noise of its scales clashing and the awful smell of its breath.

One day a knight came to Longwitton and hearing about the dragon, thought he would kill it. Hearing the story from the ploughman, he remembered he had some magic ointment that would make the invisible visible.

'From the Netherwitton fairies, no doubt,' said Harry. 'I'd rather fight a dragon than meet those people.'

The first day of fighting the dragon in the woods was fascinating. The knight turned up on a huge battle horse ('destrier'). The horse looked to Thomas like one of the carthorses he had seen at agricultural shows. The knight had masses of equipment and full armour. The lance was clearly his weapon of choice for dragon-killing. The problem was that fighting in woodland did not give the knight a good run up to the dragon. He did actually have one good thrust at the dragon and the lance went right in. Harry cheered and Thomas felt certain the dragon was done for, as blood seemed to be pouring out of an open wound.

The dragon removed the lance with its teeth and tossed it aside. Almost instantaneously, the wound appeared to heal up.

The knight was clearly mystified and rode off. The people of Longwitton were waiting for his return. They cheered as he rode into the village. You could see the embarrassment on his face as he explained the dragon was still alive.

Day two saw a change of tactics. This time the knight was lightly armoured. He still had his lance and was on a smaller, faster horse (A 'courser', according to Harry.). Before going in for his main attack, he dismounted some distance away from his dragon. He had his bow and arrows. He was clearly an expert archer. He chose his position, watched the dragon carefully, and drew his bow. He had unleashed at least six arrows in less than a minute, most of which reached their target almost certainly before the dragon realised it was being attacked.

'Well shot!' said Harry.

The knight then ran to his horse, looking extremely pleased with himself, mounted and charged at the creature with his lance.

As on the previous day, the lance went in and spouts of blood flowed out. The dragon removed the lance, the bleeding stopped and the dragon, after the fiddly task of removing the arrows, was as strong and healthy as it had ever been.

Disconsolate, the knight returned to Longwitton. A small group of villagers were waiting for him. He shook his head in answer to their questions, before dismounting.

The knight had plenty to think about. How was it that the dragon recovered so quickly from apparently fatal wounds? The great thing about this particular knight was his persistence. He was not going to give up.

He turned up the following day, lightly armoured, this time with his squire, also on horseback. His squire had spare lances and a number of additional axes and spears. Unlike the knight, who had the benefit of the magic ointment, the squire, who could not see the dragon, was only able to watch the knight and listen to the dragon.

The knight started with a quick arrow attack. The dragon moved rapidly as soon as it felt the first arrow go in. It plunged its tail in the nearby well. The knight watched carefully before returning to his horse. As before, the dragon removed the arrows using its teeth and claws, and its wounds, including the one in its eye, seemed to heal instantly.

The knight looked determined and went in for the kill with his first lance. The dragon knew what was coming and moved to avoid the attack. The knight swiftly adjusted his approach. He hit the dragon full on with his lance and it took a great deal of skill to manoeuvre his horse away from the angry beast. Spouts of blood flowed as before. The knight had quickly turned his horse around, so that he had a good view of what the dragon was doing. He saw the dragon's tail splash into the waters of the healing well and how the dragon made an immediate miraculous recovery.

He now had a plan. He rode up to his squire, who had seen very little of what had happened. They conferred. The knight took the second lance and a halberd (a sort of spiked axe on a pole).

The dragon too seemed to have formed a plan. This time, as the lance went in, it took a swipe at the knight as he turned his horse around.

The knight appeared to have been injured and seemed to fall off his horse on his way back to his squire. He had also dropped his halberd not far from where he fell. The squire, incredibly, did not move to help the knight. Somehow, the knight, despite his apparent injuries and loud groans, had regained hold of his halberd. He lay on the ground. The dragon moved forward tentatively. The knight groaned again. The squire did nothing.

The dragon's tail was now entirely clear of the well. The knight's head rolled slightly to one side as he took a good look at the dragon. He groaned again.

The dragon moved forward for the kill. Still the squire did not move. Just as the dragon reached the knight, he jumped up and gave the dragon a huge blow with the axe. Unable to reach the reviving waters of the well, it died.

As soon as it was dead, the dragon became visible to the squire, who rushed up to look at it and to congratulate the knight.

Before he woke up from his dream, Thomas saw the knight and his squire carefully fill several water bottles with water from the healing well.

CHAPTER SEVEN

St George and the Dragon

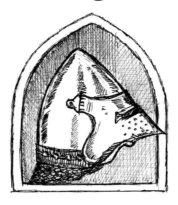

Thomas was puzzled by this dream. He had a feeling that it had a significance that somehow escaped him at the moment. He might talk to Maya about it, if he got the chance. At least she too had seen Harry and might understand why Harry was now haunting his dreams. Another thought occurred to him: 'It isn't just Harry, is it? What about the dragons?' He felt uneasy, but couldn't explain why.

That morning, when his friends called, Steve seemed transformed. He was full of laughter and energy. Thomas hardly recognised him.

'Great news! The police have cleared James!' Steve went on to say that the police now accepted that James was trying to break up the fight.

The arrest of his brother had really upset Steve and that was why he had been so quiet the previous week. Not now! Steve actually sang on the way into school and had told half a dozen really bad jokes before they reached the school gates.

Thomas said to Maya, 'Is this what he is normally like?'

Watching Steve do a cartwheel on the grass in front of the school, Maya just laughed and said, 'Yes!'

The mood at school seemed much lighter.

The dragon of the day was the one killed by St George, patron saint of England. This was a confusing sort of dragon. It seemed to involve symbolism. Was it a real dragon? Or was the whole thing really about religion?

This dragon-killing involved the rescue of a damsel. Not just any old damsel, but a princess. Miss Fairfax read them part of an old poem:

> *St. George then looking round about,*
> *The fiery dragon soon espy'd,*
> *And like a knight of courage stout,*
> *Against him did most fiercely ride*
> *And with such blows he did him greet,*
> *He fell beneath his horse's feet.*
>
> *For with his launce that was so strong,*
> *As he came gaping in his face,*
> *In at his mouth he thrust along*
> *For he could pierce no other place*
> *And thus within the lady's view*
> *This mighty dragon straight he slew.*
>
> *The savour of his poisoned breath*
> *Could do this holy knight no harm.*
> *Thus he the lady sav'd from death,*
> *And home he led her by the arm.*

Thomas thought that it was interesting that the dragon's scales were so tough that the only place St George could pierce it with his lance was through its mouth. The poisonous dragon's breath seemed to be a common hazard when tackling dragons. Plenty of material for Thomas to put in 'Myth or Monster? A Quest for the Truth about Dragons.'

He had drawn a table to summarise the information he was collecting.

The headings were: *Type of Dragon, Dragon Description, Habitat, Name of Knight, Special Equipment, Special Advisers, Weapons Used, Special Circumstances* and *Cause of Death.*

He filled out the table, putting 'princess rescue' under special circumstances, along with 'saint.'

At lunchtime, Dawn, the supervisor patrolling the playground, seemed to have lost interest in Steve. Previously she could have given the Newcastle United players lessons in man to man marking, the way she had followed Steve around at lunchtimes. This was probably due to the fact that Alan Milton and his friends had made it clear they were no longer after Steve.

Terry Milton, who had been wounded when James had tried to stop the fight, had now owned up and spoken up for him. This was why the police had dropped all the charges. It was also what the dinner ladies were talking about when Thomas, Steve and Maya went in for lunch.

'Ah heard that Kathleen Armstrong and Karen Milton, and the mothers of the other lads had aal got together and said that if their boys were old enough to go to pubs and get in fights, that they were aal old enough to give blood. They're aal gannin' down the village hall the neet to donate their blood, or their mothers'll give 'em what for.'

'Aye, well they might be keener to do it now Bobby Hedley has said he'd buy a pint for any of his regulars who donates blood.'

'That'll please them more than a cup of tea and a biscuit doon the hall.'

Steve said it was true. The mams had been on the warpath since the fight. They said if their boys wanted to shed blood they should donate some.

The manager of the Blue Lion had heard about the mams' plan and had decided to give the blood transfusion service his support too. 'He is going himself,' Steve said. 'He'll be the first in the queue.'

Thomas' mother had heard about the village mams' idea. She went down to the hall that evening to give blood herself and had waited ages in the queue. It seemed like most of the village had turned out.

When she returned home she had a long talk with Thomas. She said he must never play with or carry a knife.

'What about toy ones, Mum?'

Thomas had some plastic swords he and his dad sometimes fooled around with. They had bought them for a fancy dress party.

'I'll let you off those, son. But that's it.'

CHAPTER EIGHT

Night school

That night Thomas dreamt he was back at Alnwick Castle in the Knights' Yard. This time there was no one there except him and Harry.

Harry was looking very serious. Stacked against a wall were some shields and a variety of weapons: long swords, spears and axes of different types. There were also sacks filled with hay and some wooden swords. Tethered nearby was Harry's horse, the spirited chestnut courser.

'Welcome, Thomas Malton,' said Harry. 'By Saint George, our lady's knight, I am right glad ye have undertaken this dragon quest. I will help ye with all my power, I promise you.'

Thomas was more than a little taken aback. He did not really understand what Harry was talking about. Judging from the stack of weapons and Harry's tone of voice, he was not referring to Thomas's essay, 'Myth or Monster? A Quest for the Truth about Dragons.'

'Is this really happening?' Thomas asked. 'Isn't this a dream?'

'This is a dream and yet a time to prepare for the

encounter with the worm of Wormhill. It shall not be long ere the dragon and you meet.'

'For real?'

Harry looked at him and said steadily, 'The worm will burn Northumberland and many will lose their lives unless a champion is found. For sooth and certainly, you are the champion.'

'Harry, how do you know that I am the champion?' said Thomas,

'I was there when ye made your wish,' said Harry.

'Wish?' Then suddenly Thomas remembered what he was thinking just before he had seen Harry on the field by his school: 'I wish I had a chance to fight a dragon.'

Thomas sighed. He did not feel like arguing with the most redoubtable knight in English history. He knew that Harry had a very strong sense of honour and if he had given his word, he would abide by it. Thomas would do the same in respect of his unspoken, but evidently overheard, wish.

'Well,' he said, 'How do you prepare for fighting a fire-breathing dragon?'

Weapons training started.

Harry knew what he was about. Thomas did not understand what he was saying sometimes. Harry just repeated what he had said and demonstrated the move and Thomas followed.

They started off with thrusts and slashing movements with the different weapons. Harry gave Thomas wooden weapons to practise with first of all, then the real ones.

They attacked the hay sacks, which they had piled in the centre of the yard. Thomas knew that the dragon's hide would be much tougher. Getting used to the weight of the weapons and how to wield them to get the maximum force for each blow was what they were working on for now.

Some of the weapons took a while to get used to. The axe was one of the most tricky to handle, because of the way its weight was distributed. It needed a good swing to be effective.

The spears might be their best bet, Thomas thought. If you were close enough to the dragon to attack it with a sword, you were likely to be in extreme danger. Whatever weapon was used, it would be difficult to cut through the dragon's scales.

Now Thomas was used to the weapons, Harry decided to practise moving rapidly, attacking, and then moving swiftly before the next attack. He wanted Thomas to react to the dragon's movements. As soon as Thomas attacked, he told him which direction to move in. This simulated the dragon's unpredictable reaction.

The next phase of training involved the additional use of a shield. Thomas found that there were times it was impossible to use it. The axe, for example, needed both hands. Although the shield would protect his face, hands and top part of his body from the dragon's fiery breath, he would not be completely covered. The shield was cumbersome. Sometimes Harry would shout 'Fire!' as well as telling him which direction to move. Thomas would try to protect himself as fully as he could with the shield, as if he was protecting himself from flames.

Harry finished the training session by giving Thomas a ride on his horse. Thomas had never ridden a horse before and just mounting it took several goes. Harry didn't comment. Thomas rode slowly round the yard, just getting used to being on horseback. After two or three circuits, Harry asked Thomas to stop and dismount.

The time had come to discuss strategy.

This creature was different from the Longwitton worm. It was more deadly. Thomas, who had seen it in his dream, knew it could fly and had fire-breathing capacity. Harry nodded.

'Its very strength may prove its weakness.' Thomas did

not gain much reassurance from this comment.

The digging at the hill had wakened it.

'It will protect the dead lord and his treasure,' said Harry.

'Why don't you kill it, Harry?' asked Thomas. 'You are better at fighting than me.'

'Alas, Aah cannot kill the dragon for Aah'm a ghost,' replied Harry. 'Thou, who hast life, must slay it. It will be a marvellous deed.'

Thomas had not thought of the dragon slaying as anything other than a difficult task. He was not particularly interested in it from the point of view of glorious heroism. Harry, on the other hand, was a hero who had been brought up with tales of daring knights. For him, this adventure was what being a knight was all about.

He had sworn to protect Northumberland. The Scots had burnt Northumberland and he had fought the Scots. If the dragon tried burning Northumberland, he would face the wrath of two doughty English knights. Thomas, with Harry's help, would slay it.

Thomas, who had never killed anything in his whole life, was not too sure about any of this. He was not a knight, doughty (whatever that meant) or otherwise. Only a few hours ago, his mum had been telling him he must never carry a knife. For the last two to three hours he had been slashing holes in hay sacks with a variety of extremely sharp blades and contemplating killing a creature, which had, by his best estimate, a 99.9 per cent chance of killing him.

If the dragon had burnt down Dainty's factory as a result of the archaeologists setting up camp, heaven only knew what it would do when the dig began in earnest.

When Thomas woke up, hearing the alarm clock ring and his mother call him, he felt a sense of relief. Surely his dream had just been a dream, hadn't it?

Something was tickling his face. A long wisp of hay was caught in his hair.

CHAPTER NINE

Reconnaissance Mission

Thomas was not sure what to do. He thought about how his uncle, who was in the army, might approach the task. He would have something called an objective (such as killing the dragon). He would find out as much information as he could about the enemy. There might be a reconnaissance mission, where information was gathered about the enemy's position. Then a plan of attack would be developed. The different ways the enemy might react would be considered and tactics devised for dealing with them.

He felt that there was something he was leaving out of his thinking. The dragon was protecting something it would be prepared to die for – the burial chamber of a king. He knew Harry had risked his life many times to protect Northumberland. In that respect, they were similar.

Many people thought that burial sites were sacred. Perhaps the dragon was in the right and it was the archaeologists who were in the wrong. Was there a way of preventing the dig taking place? Couldn't the dragon and the king be left undisturbed, as they had been for centuries?

Would it be possible to capture the dragon and study it? As far as Thomas knew it might be the last of its kind. Scientific data on dragons was also non-existent.

The great difficulty was that, if he approached the people who ought to be interested (the archaeologists, the armed forces and the scientists), they would be unlikely to believe him. If he were in their shoes, he wouldn't believe a ten-year-old boy who had no evidence to support what he was saying.

Who would believe him? Maya might, as she had seen Harry. Thomas felt he had to tell someone about the dragon and the threat it posed to the area. He could tell Maya and Steve after school. Maybe if he and his friends went over to Wormhill to do some reconnaissance, they might find out some useful information about the dragon. Thomas thought that might be the best course of action.

When he went downstairs mum was listening to the news on the radio. As soon as he heard the report, Thomas knew it was the dragon.

'Berwick farmer Dave Ridley has reported that a flock of sheep have gone missing, under very mysterious circumstances. Three carcasses were left half-eaten with strange bite marks. "Mr Ridley, do you think the sheep have been attacked by dogs?"

"Ah've nivvor seen bite marks like these. That's nivvor a dog. It couldna even be a wolf. If it wa' dogs, where are the other sheep? There's nae sign of them anywhere. It's like they've vanished into thin air."

'Northumbria Police are investigating. A local vet is examining the sheep carcasses to determine what kind of animal had been eating them.'

Steve and Maya arrived. They had heard the news report. Steve jokingly said it was definitely the curse of Wormhill come true and that the worm was like the Lambton worm, fond of a few tasty lambs for its dinner.

'Did you hear the one about the two knights and the dragon, Thomas?'

Thomas felt he had heard enough about the two knights and the dragon, but didn't say anything.

'Bar-B-Q tonight! Bar-B-Q two knight, get it?'

Thomas didn't think this was at all funny, for obvious reasons.

His mum gave him a concerned look. 'Are you sure you are all right, Thomas. You look a little pale. Are you sure you're not const …'

Thomas knew what she was going to say. Whenever she thought he looked a little pale, she always said he looked constipated. She was a firm believer in old-fashioned remedies, like syrup of figs. He almost pushed Maya and Steve out the door, before she could finish.

'I'm fine, Mum. See you later!'

Outside it was still raining and there were puddles along the side of the road. Every time a car or lorry went past they had to move out of the way quickly to avoid getting soaked. It reminded Thomas of the night before and how he had to leap out of the way and cover himself with the shield every time Harry shouted 'Fire!'

He was glad to get to school. At least he could forget about Wormhill, the dragon and Harry for a few hours.

Thomas had not taken into account just how enthusiastic Miss Fairfax was about local history. She had arranged for a speaker from the university to come and talk to them about the Wormhill excavation.

The speaker was Lucinda Reid, one of the archaeology team, who said she would be working on the site, 'As soon as the rains stops!'

It was still raining heavily. Thomas hoped it went on raining for days, although that would mean no cricket for him.

Lucinda explained how they were going to excavate the hill. She was very pretty and had bright blue eyes and long curly blond hair. She showed the children some of the preliminary work that had been done, starting with some aerial photography.

Thomas stared at the slide of the aerial view. In his dream he had seen the dragon curled around the top of the hill, its body fitting exactly into the contours of the ridged pathways that circled the hill. His dream had been uncannily accurate, considering he had not seen a map or an aerial photo such as this. A chill went down his spine. More and more he was convinced that the dragon was real and his dreams had been sent to him for a reason.

Every time Lucinda turned to answer a question, her hair seemed to bounce and her dangling earrings swung about. Thomas noticed that Steve had a soppy expression on his face and seemed completely absorbed by what she was saying. There would be no difficulty in persuading him to go to Wormhill after school, for sure. If Steve thought he might see Lucinda there, he'd be there like a shot.

Steve asked her if the team had heard about the story of the dragon and if they were worried about the curse.

Lucinda laughed, a sort of light tinkling laugh, which gave Thomas the impression she thought Steve's question was amusing, rather than deadly serious.

'We have heard the story and we are fully equipped with rabbits' feet and four-leaf clovers.'

Miss Fairfax explained that in the old days people used to carry stuffed rabbits' feet that they touched for luck.

'I don't think that was very lucky for the rabbits,' said Steve.

Several of the children said they thought it was a horrible superstition. They gave the speaker some very disapproving looks. Lucinda was clearly perturbed by their reaction and the way the talk was going.

Lucinda said, 'I was just joking. We don't really have any rabbits' feet, or, for that matter, any four-leafed clovers. We have heard about the worm story. We think that it is the shape of the hill that has given rise to the legend. We are not expecting to uncover a dragon.'

'Any more questions?' asked Miss Fairfax.

'I have one,' said Thomas. 'Don't you think it is wrong to dig up a burial site? It is not very respectful.'

Lucinda had possibly not been expecting a question like this from a group of ten-year-olds. She paused, then said, 'That's a very interesting question ...' Pausing again, she asked Thomas his name, then said slowly, 'Well, Thomas, we archaeologists are very respectful of the dead. If we uncover any human remains we have to follow a very strict set of government rules and we treat the remains with care and attention to decency.

'We are not sure if Wormhill is a burial site, though we have good reasons for believing it is. We hope to learn a great deal about our ancestors as a result of this excavation.'

Thomas's was the last question. Miss Fairfax thanked Lucinda for her talk and the class gave her a round of applause.

Thomas was now in no doubt that there was little point in trying to persuade the archaeologists to end the excavation at Wormhill.

He was relieved to be doing some Maths next. It was calming and relaxing and each problem had an answer that did not require any sort of personal heroism.

By the end of the day, the rain had stopped.

It took a micro-second for Steve to agree to go to Wormhill. Maya said she would like to come too, after she had called home.

Once they arrived there, they saw that there were more tents set up in the field near to the road. There was already a crowd of people on the hill around the area that was marked out ready for excavation.

The three of them were stood at the bottom of the hill, some distance from the pathway that led up it.

'Do you think Lucinda is there?' asked Steve, looking up at the archaeologists swarming about the excavation site itself.

'Never mind Lucinda,' said Thomas. 'I wanted you both to come here because I have something to tell you about the dragon and...' He hesitated for a moment '...Harry Hotspur.'

Maya looked at him intently. Steve turned to look at Thomas.

'I haven't told you, Steve, but Maya knows already. When we went to Alnwick I saw the ghost of Harry Hotspur. I know this may seem hard to believe...'

'No, it isn't,' said Steve laughing. Thomas thought Steve was joking again, then he noticed Maya was laughing too. He felt his face turn red. 'I am trying to be serious here.' Steve and Maya started laughing hysterically.

'What's so funny?' asked Thomas.

'He's behind you!' giggled Maya.

Sure enough, Harry was standing behind him, with a huge grin on his face, enjoying the situation just as much as Steve and Maya.

Thomas did the introductions properly. He thought it would be what Harry was used to.

'Maya Patel, I would like you to meet Sir Henry Percy.'

Harry bowed elaborately. Maya smiled.

'Sir Henry Percy, I would like you to meet Steve Armstrong.'

Steve decided he would have a go at bowing and attempted to copy Harry's bow. This time it was Harry's turn to smile.

The formalities over, Thomas briefed Maya and Steve about the dragon.

'I thought we might be able to find out more about the dragon by coming here,' said Thomas. 'For one thing, how it gets in and out of the hill, if that is where it lives.'

There was quite a lot of noise coming from the hill at this point. The team had brought a small digger up the path and had started to remove some of the turf. They were also putting some fencing around the site to keep the public off it.

Suddenly the ground appeared to shake. Thomas thought he heard a muffled roar. The fencing fell over. The digger rolled over and slid down the hill. Most of the people on the hill had fallen over. No one appeared to be injured.

Thomas was certain he could smell smoke in the air. People hurried down the slope of the hill.

Harry had disappeared.

Scores of mud-covered people were descending the hill.

'It must be an earthquake,' said a woman in an anorak, waterproof trousers and green wellies. It was Lucinda. Wiping some mud off her face, she said, 'We had better move everyone away from the hill in case there are aftershocks.' The man she was with agreed. 'Let's get everyone off the hill, now.'

'Not much chance of us having a look around then,' said Steve.

'Where's Harry?' asked Maya.

'He's gone,' said Thomas.

They walked back home. All three were convinced that the dragon had roared and had made the earth shake.

'Won't the archaeologists stop now?' asked Maya.

'Well, you heard what Lucinda said,' Thomas replied. 'They will go on believing it's an earthquake until it's too late.'

'What do you mean, too late?'

'Until they see the dragon for themselves. Then it will be too late for them,' said Thomas grimly.

CHAPTER TEN

Whose dream is this anyway?

That night Thomas found it hard to go to sleep. There was too much to think about. Eventually, when he did fall asleep, he found himself at Alnwick Castle, in the Knights' Yard. This didn't surprise him at all. Nothing much about his dreams would surprise him now, he thought.

He was wrong. In the middle of the yard, already busy with training, were Maya and Steve. They were each holding a shield and spear.

'Fire! Right!' yelled Harry. They covered themselves with the shields and darted swiftly to the right. 'Attack!' They launched their spears at the dragon, represented by the pile of sacks of hay.

'What kept you?' asked Steve. 'We've been here ages. Now you are here, welcome to my dream!'

Now Thomas joined them as they practised taking it in turns to attack different sides of the 'dragon'. The idea was to never let it know where the next attack was coming from.

They stopped for a while to discuss tactics.

'We need to think about what we know about the dragon and how best to defeat it,' said Maya.

'Have you seen the dragon, Harry?'

'Aye. Aah've seen it. So has Thomas. Ye had a good look at it, Thomas. Tell Maya and Steve what you saw.'

'I saw it in a dream, like this one. It is huge. The main part of its body is about the size of the school minibus, but its neck is long and its tail can wind around the top of Wormhill several times. It has wings and I am sure it could fly, although I didn't see it fly. I saw it breathe out fire. First it made a sort of rattling noise and then a sort of hissing sound and then it belched flames and smoke.'

'We could really do with a tank against a monster like that,' said Steve. Harry looked puzzled, but did not say anything.

'Yeah, well, we haven't got one,' said Thomas.

'Meyybes once people know it's there, the army might use one against it.'

'Meyybes a lot of people will be dead by then, and a lot of homes burnt.'

'Knights like St George and Sir Launcelot didn't have tanks,' said Maya. 'They did all right against dragons.'

'Were any of them fire-breathing dragons?'

'I read a story about the one Sir Launcelot killed. It spit fire, and lived in a tomb. It took him a long time but he did kill it.'

'How?'

'It didn't say how. It just said it was difficult.'

There was a silence. Thomas said, 'Well, what do we know about dragons' weaknesses?'

'They are supposed to be fond of gold. They hoard it,' said Maya.

'And fond of damsels,' added Steve.

'I am sure I read somewhere they like riddles,' said Steve.

'That's all right then,' said Thomas. 'You can make it laugh itself to death.'

'Perhaps we could use some gold to distract it,' said Maya. 'You know, take its eye off the ball.'

'What do ye mean, take its eye off the ball?' asked Harry.

Thomas looked at Harry. How could he explain it?

'You explain it, Steve,' he said. 'It's your dream.'

'Is it my dream? I thought it was your dream.'

'I don't care whose dream it is,' said Maya. 'Let's show Harry what we mean. Let's pretend my trainer is a piece of the dragon's hoard.'

She got up and went over towards the stack of hay sacks, then put the trainer down. Then said, 'There's a piece of the dragon's treasure. Steve, you get ready to attack.'

She picked up the trainer and waved it. 'Here nasty dragon, look what I've got! A piece of your precious treasure!'

Steve said, 'While Maya has its attention, I kill it like this.' He stuck the spear into the hay.

After that they did some axe practice. There were sacks of turnips to practice on. The axes were heavy. Maya never really managed to get a good swing with hers. Steve seemed to be able to wield his with some force. None of them particularly liked the axe as a weapon.

Harry gave Steve and Maya a ride each on his horse. Neither of them had ever ridden a horse before. Maya sat well on the horse, though she did have some difficulty getting it to move.

Harry did not comment. Thomas noticed that the lance, propped up against the wall was the one weapon they had not tried. You needed to be a skilled rider to use the lance effectively.

It was time to go. Thomas thought he heard the faint sound of alarm clocks going off, somewhere in the distance.

Then suddenly first Maya, then Steve disappeared from the yard.

Thomas looked briefly at Harry. A second later, he was waking up to the loud sound of his own alarm clock going off.

Maya

CHAPTER ELEVEN

Cricket on the park

It was Friday and Dad would be back from Leeds tonight. It was a bright sunny morning. Perfect! Thomas forgot about the dragon and his dreams for a moment or two and suddenly felt great. The weather was just right for cricket on the park.

Mum seemed much happier too. She was singing along to the radio when he came downstairs. Normally, Thomas would have groaned and asked her to stop. Today he crept up on her and joined in, which made her jump. They both laughed.

Maya and Steve arrived. Steve had a newspaper, which as soon as they were out of the house, he showed to Thomas. Thomas looked at the headline: 'Evaporated Milk!' He gave Steve a puzzled look.

'Read it!' said Steve, impatiently.

> *A bizarre accident involving a Flannan Dairies milk tanker took place at Stannington, near Morpeth, yesterday. No one was injured, but the*

tanker was overturned and traffic was held up for several hours while the police investigated the incident.

No other vehicle was involved in the incident. Police confirm that the tanker appeared to have been overturned as a result of freak weather conditions. Inexplicably, the side of the tanker appears to have been ripped open and the contents, a full load of milk, have disappeared. 'It looked as if a giant can opener had made a massive gash in the side of the tanker,' said a resident of Station Road, Bill Wallace, 62. 'Nearly all of the milk had gone. Only a very small amount was left. It is a mystery as to where it has disappeared.'

The driver, Wilf Gibson, 43, has been taken to hospital suffering from shock. Mark Simpson, 31, who had stopped to offer the driver assistance, said Mr Gibson had said he had not seen anything. 'In fact, that was what seemed to upset him the most.'

A spokesman from the Met Office confirmed that a mini-tornado might possibly cause such an accident, but was unable to comment on this particular case.

Related stories:

Freak lightning strike has been blamed for the Dainty's factory fire on Monday. Fire Investigator Baffled. See page 6.

Recent heavy rainfalls may be the explanation for the Wormhill earth tremor. Land Slip Halts Dig. See page 5.

'It's the dragon again. I am sure of it.'

Thomas considered the story. 'The milk bit reminds me of the Lambton worm, for sure.'

He did not say any more. What he was thinking was that

the beast must be extraordinarily powerful to overturn the tanker. Would spiky armour help a knight defeat a creature who was able to rip open the side of a steel milk tanker? He didn't think it would.

Another rather unpleasant thought occurred to him.

If the creature followed the pattern of the Lambton worm, eating sheep and drinking milk, it wouldn't be long before it started to 'swally little bairns alive'.

At school, they were nearing the end of their Lambton worm lessons. They listened to a version of the poem in standard English. Somehow it did not seem as exciting as the older versions they had heard.

Thomas turned to his essay, 'Myth or Monster? A Quest for the Truth about Dragons.' He considered his first question: 'If dragons never existed, why are there so many stories about them?' If dragons could choose to be invisible, like the Longwitton dragon and the one under Wormhill, then that might explain a great deal.

The part of the essay he was currently working on was about how dragons had been defeated in the past. He had decided to include the mythical story of Perseus and Andromeda and the sea monster. It was a good example of how a hero rescued a damsel in distress. The special equipment in this case was the Gorgon Medusa's head, which turned anything that looked at it into stone. It had taken Perseus a great deal of trouble and enormous courage to obtain the head.

He kept thinking about the Wormhill dragon. Since Harry had told him that he was destined to fight the dragon, he had thought of very little else. Thinking about it logically, he felt very gloomy about his prospects of defeating a fire-breathing dragon. Harry had shown him some sword, axe and spear basics. Thomas's research indicated that successful knights had used special equipment, careful observations, guile and information from a wise old woman to defeat their various scaly adversaries.

What did he have, which would help him defeat such a dreadful enemy? He couldn't think of anything and felt very despondent. He wasn't alone though. He did have friends. Friends, who seeing his sad face, made a real effort to cheer him up. It was lunchtime, so they went outside to play football.

The afternoon went by very slowly. Thomas was looking forward to his dad's return and the game of cricket. He had already asked Steve and Maya if they would like to play and they said they would.

Eventually it was half past three and school was over.

When Thomas arrived home, Dad was back. He had already put the cricket gear in his sports bag and was irritating Mum by practising bowling swings in the lounge, while she was trying to do the ironing. Maya and Steve agreed to meet at the park in about half an hour.

The park was busy. It was a warm afternoon and people were taking advantage of it. Families were playing with Frisbees, children were playing football and dogs were barking and chasing balls thrown by their owners. The park felt normal and safe.

They found a quiet spot over the far side of the park and set up the stumps. Thomas practised bowling against his dad with a real cricket ball. At school they played quick cricket with a soft ball. Thomas much preferred the real thing. Maya and Steve turned up. Dad thought it would be better to use a tennis ball now and Thomas put the proper ball in his jacket pocket.

They were having a lot of fun when Alan and his gang arrived and stood watching them.

'Why don't you ask your friends to play?' suggested Dad, nodding to where the boys were.

'They go to my school, but they're not exactly my friends, Dad.'

'Well, you never know, they might be.'

Dad shouted over, 'Do you want to join in?'

With more people playing, it was much better.

Everyone had a turn to bat and bowl. Alan was quite a good batsman and it took ages to get him out. Steve bowled him out in the end. David caught Maya's hooked shot, jumping up and stretching out to reach it. It was an amazing catch and even Maya, who was out first ball, applauded. Dad did some silly run-ups to bowl to Thomas, which made everyone laugh.

All too soon it was time to go home. Alan, David and Martin were now on good terms with Thomas and his friends. Dad had been right to ask them to play. Thomas had had such a good time that two hours had passed quickly without him even thinking once about the dragon quest.

CHAPTER TWELVE

Smite the dragon!

The dream-time weapons practice was very similar to the previous night. The main difference was that Harry introduced a new tactic. 'Keep its ee frae the baal!'

The first time Harry said it, Thomas, Maya and Steve looked at each other. Each knew the others wanted to laugh, but they restrained themselves and got on with it.

What happened was, one of them would pick up a turnip and throw it over the dragon, while another scurried in and dealt it a blow. Harry encouraged them to shout at the dragon as they threw the turnip.

Harry was learning some of their words and they were learning some of his. They were picking up a few new words, such as 'buffet', which meant blow, and 'smite', which meant strike.

They were practising cutting, slashing and thrusting moves, as well as some spear throwing. Harry was concentrating on what would be useful against the dragon.

He did not attempt to teach them archery, or jousting, or hand to hand combat skills, all of which would take a long time to learn properly.

He seemed to be very religious and when he became serious and he was talking about the fight with the dragon itself, he would begin what he was saying by referring to Jesus, or Our Lady, or Saint George. Harry knew the task was perilous and that they were risking their lives, though he did not say so directly.

Thomas was not sure whether Maya or Steve understood how dangerous the dragon was. Of the three of them, he was the only one who had seen it, albeit in a dream. It was not going to be like a computer game, where if you were killed by the dragon you had another life and could attempt to kill it again, or you could switch the game off and play something else. Perhaps he was underestimating them and the others were just braver than he was. He didn't know.

Maya and Steve were here because of their friendship with him. If anything happened to them, he would be responsible. This feeling of responsibility was a new experience for him. It was hard. Maybe facing up to this was worse than facing the dragon itself.

He would soon find out, that was for sure.

When he woke up, he felt as if a weight had been taken from his shoulders. It was Saturday and he was home, where he felt safe.

It would be his first session at the Judo club that morning and he was looking forward to it.

He was not the only newcomer. Alan Milton had decided he would like to learn. Not surprisingly, since he had not got over the shock of being thrown by Maya. His friends had kept on about how he had been thrown by a girl, so he had not been allowed to forget it either.

Most of the time at Judo was spent learning break falls. From time to time he and Alan would stop and watch the others who were practising throws. Thomas learned a little bit about the ideas behind the 'gentle way' of judo. By giving way, an opponent's force could be used against that person.

Thomas immediately started to wonder how this might apply to the dragon, which was far more powerful than him and his friends were. He remembered Harry's words: 'Its very strength may prove its weakness.'

When Thomas got back home, lunch was nearly ready. Mum had made a fish pie, which was one of Dad's favourites.

Over lunch, Mum started talking about the dig. She said that she had heard it was due to restart today and she wouldn't mind going to have a look. Thomas nearly choked at this point. His mum started fussing over him, worried that he might have a fish bone lodged in his throat or something. Thomas said he was fine.

His dad said he was gong to watch the local football team take on the Bedlington Terriers. 'It should be good for a laugh. Do you want to come, Thomas?'

Thomas really did not want his mum to go to Wormhill, especially by herself. He looked at her and said, 'I will if you will, Mum.'

'Ok then,' said his mum. 'It will be nice to go together as a family.'

Thomas felt relieved. His mum would be much safer at the match.

Until it was time to go, Thomas and his dad had an impromptu sword-fight with the plastic swords.

'Have at thee, villain,' said his dad very theatrically.

Thomas fought back, trying to avoid dad's sword and reach past it to pretend to run him through. Dad countered this move and succeeded in getting his sword under Thomas's throat.

'Yield!'

'Never!' replied Thomas, ducking down and moving out of his dad's reach.

His mum put her head round the kitchen door. 'Would you like leg of lamb for Sunday lunch tomorrow, John? I'll have to take it out of the freezer if you do.'

'Aye. That'll be champion. There is nothing like a nice Sunday roast.'

Thomas winced at his father's turn of phrase. He was worried he might be the roast for the dragon's Sunday lunch. His dad seized the opportunity and pretended to run him through.

'You're now officially dead, Thomas. I definitely got you that time.'

Thomas said he had had enough sword fighting. Sometimes he thought Dad was just like a big kid. He just had to win.

They put their coats on and went off to the match.

At half time, the family went for some tea. It was quite chilly that afternoon for late spring, so they thought hot drinks were a good idea. Thomas asked his parents what they knew about Harry Hotspur.

'Well, I know he was a famous knight who was born in Alnwick Castle. He was one of the Percy family. Did you know Tottenham Hotspur was named after him? Apparently they used to have a house and land down there, near where the football ground is now. That's why the club got its name.'

'When I was at school they told us about the Battle of Otterburn,' said his mum. 'The Scots had attacked Northumberland, burning many towns and villages. Percy was in the castle at Newcastle, along with his wife. The two commanders decided to fight each other in front of the castle.

The Scottish leader, Earl Douglas, and Harry Percy fought on horseback. Percy received an injury from Douglas's spear.' ('Was this a lance?' Thomas wondered. He thought it would make more sense if it were.)

His mother continued: 'His wife, who was on the battlements, saw the whole thing and was very upset by it.

Anyway, Percy said he would meet up with Douglas three days later to finish the fight. Douglas would be at Otterburn.

Hotspur knew that there were reinforcements on the way to him, but he had given Douglas his word that he would fight him three days later. His pride did not allow him to wait until it was sensible to attack. He had made a promise and he would keep it, wounded or not.

The English forces were hopelessly outnumbered. Hotspur led the attack. He fought Earl Douglas in hand to hand combat and killed him. He himself was captured by the Scots and held to ransom. Many of his brave followers had died in that battle.'

Thomas thought about the reality of fighting and how Harry from a young age had taken part in battles and seen friends and relatives die at the hands of the Scots. His dad told him that in those times, if you came from a family like Harry's, you were trained for fighting from as young as five or six. Harry's dad had Harry taken to the battlefield when he was eight. The Earl of Northumberland would have made sure that his son Harry was well protected. Still, Harry would have seen sights on the field of battle that Thomas could not even imagine. 'Sights I couldn't imagine, either. Those were very different times, son.'

They went back to watch the second half. The match was a good one, considering the teams were just amateurs. The Terriers won by three goals to one. The Maltons headed for home.

The dreamtime training session at Alnwick Castle now seemed routine. They were practising the moves that they had learnt and developing team strategies for fighting the dragon.

They talked about armour. Apart from shields, they decided they didn't want armour. It might not be much help against a dragon that could breathe fire. They weren't used to wearing it and they thought it might slow them down.

Moving quickly against a bigger, stronger opponent was one advantage they felt they had.

Another advantage was that they would work as a team and look out for each other.

There was a sense of urgency about the practice. They all felt that it would not be long before they would confront the dragon. The next day they were going to meet and have a look round Wormhill. They were going to try to find its lair. It had to be somewhere under the hill and the dragon had to be getting in and out somehow.

Maya disappeared from the dream first. Thomas was almost sure he could hear her cat making a strange crying sound as she vanished. Then Steve disappeared, with a loud alarm clock noise in the background.

It was morning.

A few minutes after Thomas had woken up, Harry appeared in his room.

'It's Maya,' he said. 'The worm has captured her.'

'You are sure she hasn't been ...' Thomas gulped, thinking of the Lambton Worm, '... swallowed?'

'Not yet.'

CHAPTER THIRTEEN

Damsel in Distress

Thomas got dressed hurriedly. Harry would meet him outside, where his horse was waiting.

Thomas's parents were having breakfast early, as his dad was for going for a Sunday morning run.

'Toast?' offered his dad.

'I hope not,' shuddered Thomas, thinking of Maya. He told his parents he would have breakfast later. He gave Mum a hug before he went to the door.

'Where are you off to in such a hurry?' asked his dad.

'I'm off to Wormhill to kill the dragon,' said Thomas, who was certain his parents wouldn't believe him.

'Oh well, that's all right then,' said his dad, laughing. 'See you later!'

Harry was on his horse. He pulled Thomas up behind him and they set off for Steve's. On the way, Harry explained that after Thomas left Alnwick Castle, Harry had seen the dragon. It flew slowly over the castle with someone held in its claws. Then a shoe dropped from the sky, almost at his feet. He produced one of Maya's trainers from a pocket by the saddle. When Harry saw the trainer, he recognised it as Maya's and he knew for sure that the dragon had Maya. Harry was certain the dragon had flown over the Knights' Yard so that he would see it. 'It knows we have accepted its challenge. It will be waiting for us at Wormhill.'

Thomas thought the dragon was deliberately taunting them. His blood ran cold at the thought that Maya was in its clutches.

When they reached Steve's house, they found Steve just about to leave. He had just got on his bike ready to go to the newsagent's. Steve nearly fell off when he saw them both, in broad daylight, sat on the horse, which was trotting towards him.

'It's Maya!' said Thomas. 'The dragon has got her!'

Steve cycled after them. It was very early in the morning and no one seemed to be about to see them.

When they arrived at Wormhill, all seemed to be quiet. The archaeologists were probably still sound asleep in their tents.

Round the other side of the hill, they saw another horse, tethered by the gate, loaded up with shields and weapons. Harry, somehow, had sent it ahead.

What they saw next, or rather did not see, surprised them.

'It's gone!' said Steve.

'How on earth could it just go?' asked Thomas.

The turf maze, which had been there for centuries, had just vanished. There was no sign of it. The field was just a field like any other. The spring was still there, bubbling away near to the hill.

Steve, Harry and Thomas then started their search. Where had the dragon taken Maya? They felt there must be an entrance to the hill somewhere. They started scouring the hill, looking for clues.

Suddenly Thomas heard a shout. It was Steve.

He had found one of Maya's trainers beside some bushes, near the spring. 'It's definitely Maya's,' said Steve. 'Look, it matches the other one.'

They searched the bushes. The earth seemed to have been disturbed. Then they found a large carved stone, set in the hillside.

'It won't budge,' said Steve. 'I am sure this is the entrance.

'How are we going to get inside?'

CHAPTER FOURTEEN

Dead or Alive?

Almost as soon as he had seen the spiral design on the stone, Thomas knew exactly what he had to do. The stone was carved with raised circles spiralling from the centre. Strangely, the surface looked as if it were new and the craftsman had just finished making it. He pressed the centre circle and started counting on and pressing the centre of circles. 'Zero, one, one, two, three, five, eight'. As he touched the circles, using the Fibonacci sequence, he felt the stone start to move. He counted on thirteen circles. 'Thirteen', then 'Twenty-one'. The stone moved each time that he pressed the next circle in the sequence. By the time he reached thirty-four, the slab rolled sideways and there was just enough space to go inside what looked like a tunnel.

Steve was amazed. 'How did you know to do that? That was like magic.'

'It's Maths,' said Thomas. 'It's easy.'

The three of them peered inside the opening. The tunnel was formed out of rock and curved away to the left.

Thomas caught Steve's eye. 'Tactics,' said Steve.

They looked at each other. It would be sensible to go over these one final time.

Thomas said, 'We need to rescue Maya. That's what's most important. The dragon can't attack all of us at the same time, so we need to split up and keep separate from each other.

'We must go in quietly and try not to alert it. Once it knows we are there, we must try to distract it while we rescue Maya.

'We need to keep moving. It can easily burn us or crush us. Understood?'

Steve and Harry nodded sombrely.

Harry unpacked the weapons and shields from the second horse. They each had a shield with the Percy lion, long sword and a couple of spears. Remembering the Longwitton dragon, Thomas asked Steve to fill the water bottle from his bike with water from the spring. Thomas was about put it in his jacket pocket, when he found he had still got the cricket ball from yesterday in there. He put the bottle in his left pocket instead.

Steve and Thomas tested the weight of their weapons, getting used to the feel of them. They would soon be putting them to use.

'You opened the door, Thomas, so you should have the honour of leading,' said Harry. He looked at Thomas and Steve. 'You must win your spurs today,' he said quietly.

Harry gestured towards the tunnel.

Thomas went first, clutching his shield, spears and sword. As he entered the darkness, he whispered 'Esperance!' and he heard the others repeat it softly too, as they followed.

As they moved along the gloomy tunnel, the walls curved round. Thomas realised he was following a spiral into the hillside. The tunnel was not completely dark, as torches burnt at intervals along the side of the tunnel. The air was smokey and seemed to be getting warmer the further they went into the tunnel. There seemed to a rumbling sound reverberating along the tunnel. Briefly, Thomas wondered if the disappearance of the turf maze outside was linked to the appearance of this spiral tunnel inside the hill. The tunnel gave him an eerie feeling. He felt as if he was moving not just through space, but also through something supernatural, something which part of his brain recognised, but the part that was doing his conscious thinking refused to acknowledge or understand. How, for example, had the torches got there? Why hadn't they burnt out? 'Maybe I'll have time to think about that if we get out alive,' he thought.

Each turn of the spiral was leading them closer to where the dragon was waiting. The main difficulty they would have, he realised, was getting out again. There was only one exit. The dragon could easily keep them from escaping.

Thomas felt his heart pounding faster. His mouth was dry.

The atmosphere was becoming steadily smokier, hotter and fouler and the walls became more curved. He guessed the centre of the maze was round the next turn. The rumbling noise had grown louder. He could not think what it could be, other than the dragon. Now there was an awful smell, sort of like dog's breath, meaty and intense. It reminded him of a sort of rancid roast lamb smell as well, possibly with an additional whiff of smoke from a coal fire.

He gripped the spear and long sword more tightly.

No amount of lessons on the Lambton worm or dreams about dragons could have prepared him for what he saw as he turned round the corner.

It was a ship burial all right – the archaeologists had guessed correctly. The ship looked as if it had been placed there yesterday. There was treasure scattered all over the floor of the cavernous space at the centre of the hill. An enamelled dragon stared up from the shield that lay on the ground in front of him.

Thomas looked up at the real dragon, which was huge and was coiled around the ship. The main part of its green, scaly body was about the size of a mini-bus, but its length was enormous. Its powerful tail would be a force to be reckoned with. The dragon was sleeping, with its head on the front of the ship.

The prow of the ship had a brightly painted wooden dragon's head jutting from it. The red–rimmed eyes glared evilly at him. No wonder the dragon felt at home here, with his wooden pal to keep him company.

The stench seemed to be emanating from the dragon's mouth. It was its foul breath. The now deafening, echoing, rumbling noise was its snoring. With each vile breath a large gold cup rolled to and fro, directly in front of the dragon.

The king, in full armour, lay in the middle of the ship. Thomas saw that the corpse looked newly dead. The chief's long blond hair was visible below the helmet that covered his head and most of his face. His pale skin and blue lips could just be seen under the bronze of the helmet. Time must have stood still, here in the centre of Wormhill.

Where was Maya?

Thomas scanned the cavern anxiously and saw that Maya was slumped near a heap of treasure, on the other side of the ship, by a deep crack in the rocky floor. She wasn't burnt, thank goodness. She was wearing pink pyjamas and her feet were bare. The dragon must have snatched her from her house.

Steve and Harry had joined him. Thomas signalled that he was going over to Maya. As he moved quietly towards her, he saw no signs of movement. A dreadful thought crossed his mind. Was she dead?

CHAPTER FIFTEEN

Earth, Wind, Fire, Water

Thomas looked at Maya anxiously.

Maya looked pale, seemed to be unconscious, but was breathing.

He wedged one of his spears into the crack in the rocky floor. It was tilted towards the dragon and might offer some protection if the dragon moved towards them. He knelt down next to Maya, keeping a wary eye on the sleeping dragon.

Thomas took the water bottle from his pocket and gently splashed some water on her face. He was relieved when Maya opened her eyes and smiled at him. She drank some of the water. She didn't say anything, but looked at the dragon and then at him. 'Maybe the spring has healing powers, like the Longwitton wells,' thought Thomas, as Maya quickly rose to her feet.

They were just about to move towards the exit when the dragon opened its huge yellow eyes. Thomas and Maya froze.

It raised its head towards them. They could feel its warm smokey breath directed towards them. Thomas gripped his sword tightly. He felt certain it would attack.

Just then Steve shouted 'Hey!' The noise echoed around the cavern. He had picked up a large gold plate from the floor in front of him. He threw it across the cavern towards Harry. The plate span like a giant shiny Frisbee. Harry caught it and threw it back to Steve, who ran to catch it. For a few moments it was almost like a game of pig in the middle, with the dragon twisting and turning as it followed the flight of the plate. Suddenly the dragon's throat made a rattling sound, followed by a hissing sound. Thomas knew what that meant. He shouted 'Fire! Right!' Steve threw his spear straight into the dragon's mouth just as it was about to spit flames. He covered himself with his shield and darted behind a large boulder by the tunnel entrance. Thomas held his breath. Was Steve all right? The rock seemed for a moment to be engulfed in flames.

The dragon roared with a noise so loud that the whole of the cavernous burial chamber seemed to vibrate. Green blood oozed out of the side of its mouth. Steve's spear had wounded it.

Even the dead king's body had seemed to stir, such was the terrible echoing noise. Thomas had heard the phrase 'Loud enough to wake the dead' before. It hadn't meant anything until now. With horror, he saw the dead king reach for his sword, stand up and start to advance on Harry. Harry was ready for him. From the far side of the cave, the swacking of swords could be heard. The most renowned fourteenth century English knight was taking on a sixth century Saxon king.

Thomas saw movement behind the rock. Steve was alive! He could not tell if Steve was injured and he had not time for more than a swift glance.

The dragon was turning towards Maya and Thomas once

more. Thomas gave Maya the shield. There was no cover on this side of the ship burial and the shield might give her some protection against the dragon's fiery breath. Then he threw his spear at the dragon. He thought its throat might be a weak spot. The spear bounced off its scales and clattered to the floor without causing the dragon any harm. Thomas was in a desperate situation. His second spear was still in the crack in the rock front of him and there wasn't time to retrieve it. His sword would not be much use against the flames of the dragon's breath. Again he heard the rattle of the creature's throat and the strange hissing noise.

He heard himself shout 'Fire! Left!'

He thought that if he went one way and Maya the other, at least one of them might stand a chance of surviving. He paused, not really understanding what his brain was telling him to do. With a flash of inspiration, he reached in his pocket for the cricket ball. He aimed it directly at the dragon's eye. It hit the glaring yellow eye and stayed embedded in it. The dragon stopped hissing and staggered back, then lunged towards them furiously, smoke billowing from its nostrils.

'Thomas! Run!' shouted Steve. 'Right!'

Thomas leapt to the right. He heard a crashing noise behind him and a terrifying, agonised roar.

Thomas had forgotten about the spear. In its fury, the dragon had not noticed it either. The huge beast impaled itself on the spear. Blood spouted from its wound and it lashed its tail madly. The sticky green dragon's blood foamed and bubbled corrosively as it touched the floor.

Suddenly the monster fell forward. Just in time, Thomas moved out of its way as it crashed to the floor. It was dead. With a great sighing noise, its last breath left its body.

Steve joined Thomas as he stared at the enormous creature. Thomas looked up. To his great relief, Steve was completely unharmed, not even singed. Maya dropped the shield she was holding and ran to give Steve and Thomas a hug.

'Well, that's one in the eye for the dragon!'

Thomas felt completely drained and wondered how Steve was able to make a joke at a time like this.

'It's a talent,' laughed Steve. Just then a cold wind seemed to rush through the cavern.

'Where's Harry?' asked Thomas.

The sound of swords clashing had ceased abruptly. The dragon, Harry and the borrowed weapons suddenly vanished. The body of the king was back in the ship and seemed to have shrunk and rotted away. Its skull grinned at them under the elaborate bronze and gilt helmet.

The walls of the cavern were closing in. There was a creaking, grinding noise as the rocks seemed to move.

'Run!'

Maya pushed both boys towards the entrance. They ran faster than they ever thought they possibly could. By the time they tumbled out through the entrance, they were gasping for breath. 'Look out!' yelled Maya, this time pulling the boys out of the way. A section of the hill above the entrance seemed to move and a huge mudslide covered what had been the entrance to the tunnel. At a safe distance, they were amazed as the hill appeared to rearrange itself and settle down.

After all the noise of the wind and the tunnel closing in on them and the landslide, everything seemed suddenly very peaceful. The sun was shining, the air smelt incredibly fresh and there were birds singing in the trees that edged the field. A blackbird hopped about investigating the newly bare earth not far from where they lay, sprawled out on the grass.

'I thought we were supposed to have been rescuing you,' said Thomas, extremely grateful yet again for Maya's quick reflexes.

'You saved us just now, Maya.'

He noticed Maya's trainers, where they had left them beside the spring.

'Your shoes, Madam,' he said, bowing and presenting them to her.

'I am glad you found them,' said Maya. 'I knew you would come looking for me. I kicked one off over the Knights' Yard and the other off when I saw the entrance to the hill.' Once again, Thomas marvelled at Maya's presence of mind. If he had been held in dragon's vicious clutches, he doubted if he would have done the same.

'How did the dragon capture you?' he asked.

'When I woke I heard Smokey, my cat, making a racket outside, so I got up, put on my trainers and went to let him in before he woke everyone else up. The dragon must have been flying overhead and when it spotted me, swooped down and grabbed me. There wasn't much I could do as it was holding me so tightly in its claws. Smokey knew it was there, which is why he was making such a noise.

'It was scary flying above all the houses. I thought it might drop me, especially when it flew over the castle. I managed to kick off one of the trainers over the Knights' Yard. I hoped Harry would realise that the dragon had captured me. When we got to the hill, the entrance seemed to open of its own accord. I knew you might not find it easily, so I left the other trainer as a clue. When I saw the entrance close up again, I was very glad I did.

'The dragon seemed to rush through the tunnel. When it got to the ship, it just let go of me.

'I can't remember much of what happened in the centre of the hill. I think I passed out inside the cave because of the heat and the horrible smell.'

'What time is it?' asked Thomas, who hadn't a watch.

'It's only eight o' clock,' said Steve. 'I'd better get to the newsagent's to do the round. I am really late.'

'I'd better get home before my parents notice I'm not

there,' said Maya, shivering. It was cold, despite the early morning sunshine.

Thomas gave Maya his jacket. It wasn't all that warm and she was in pink cotton pyjamas printed with a teddy bear design.

They walked past the maze, which had mysteriously reappeared exactly where it had always been. Thomas wondered if its disappearance had co-incided with the appearance of the supernatural spiral tunnel inside the hill.

The archaeologists were up and about in the next field, busy cooking their breakfasts over small camping stoves. He started to feel hungry himself when he smelt the aroma of bacon and eggs drifting his way.

'How was Harry doing against the king?' Thomas asked.

'From what I saw, he was doing really well,' said Steve. 'He certainly kept the king busy and well away from us. I don't think we could have fought against the king as well as the dragon.'

'The dragon was bad enough on its own,' said Maya. 'Why do you think its body vanished?'

'Who knows?' said Thomas. 'The whole hill seemed to change when the dragon died. Maybe the curse was broken, I don't know.'

'Where did Harry go?' asked Steve. 'Do you think we will ever see him again?'

These were two questions for which Thomas had no answers.

CHAPTER SIXTEEN

When a knight won his spurs...

Sunday passed reasonably quietly after that, although Thomas really did not feel like eating the roast lamb and mint sauce at lunchtime. It reminded him strongly of the dragon's breath, which was something he preferred not to think about while eating.

His mother gave him a concerned look.

'It's ok, Mum. It looks very nice, but I just don't feel like it today.'

He ate up his vegetables, even the cabbage, which he normally resisted, in the hope it would stop her worrying. This, of course, worried her even more.

'You do look pale, Thomas. Are you sure you're not const...'

At this point Thomas's Dad, seeing a look of despair settling on his son's face and guessing which way the conversation was heading, gallantly attempted to change the topic of conversation.

'Lizzie, I am sure the lad is fine. I have some good news I want to tell you both.'

Dad, who had been to the pub for a quick pint before lunch, had a conversation with a local farmer, who was starting a business bottling the spring water from Wormhill and selling it. He had offered him a job setting up and managing the bottling plant.

'He is going to build a new factory on the site of the old Dainty's building, if he can get the land for a good price.'

Thomas, who had seen the reviving benefits of the spring water on Maya earlier that day, thought that bottling it and selling it as mineral water was a great idea.

Weeks and months passed by and Dad was now managing the new mineral water plant and was earning more money than he had when at Dainty's. He had even bought a new car.

From time to time, Thomas was reminded of his adventure. One morning, when Maya and Steve arrived to walk with him to school, they were laughing hysterically. Steve passed him a copy of the local paper and pointed at the headline: 'Howzat! Archaeologists stumped by cricket ball!'

The dig had uncovered a cricket ball in the middle of the ship burial at Wormhill. The archaeologists were puzzled as to how it had got there but had concluded that it was some sort of prank by one of their team, but no-one was prepared to own up to it.

Further on in the article it mentioned that the treasures from the site were to be displayed in a specially built Heritage Centre. This, it was hoped, would create more local jobs and bring visitors to the area. Thomas kept the paper as a reminder, in case he started to think the whole adventure had been a dream.

It was coming up to his birthday and his dad asked him what he would like to do on the actual day, which was a Saturday.

Thomas knew exactly what we wanted to do.

'I'd like to visit Alnwick Castle again.'

His dad agreed to take him and he also said Maya and Steve could come too. On the way to Alnwick Dad kept on making jokes. He and Steve were a right pair.

'What do you get when you cross a monkey with the ocean?' asked Steve.

'I don't know. What do you get when you cross a monkey with the ocean?'

'A chimp and sea! Chimpanzee!' Everyone groaned except Dad and Steve who kept trying to out-do each other.

'We might meet the duke at the castle,' said his dad, 'That is, if his dukiness is in.'

'It's not his dukiness,' said Maya. 'I am sure it's His Grace.'

'I've never met him,' said Steve, 'but I know he wouldn't be called Grace. That's a girl's name.'

They stopped at the statue of Harry Hotspur on the way to the Knights' Yard. Thomas's parents strolled ahead, while the others looked up at the figure on horseback.

'That's him?' said Steve, indicating the statue.

'Yes,' said Thomas. 'And this is where I first saw Harry.'

'Do you think we might see him again, now we are here?' asked Maya.

'I wish we could see him once more,' said Thomas. 'I don't know if we will, though.'

They went into the yard, looking about curiously, just in case Harry was there.

Maya never wore dresses and Steve and Thomas were amazed when she decided to dress up in one of the ladies' costumes. 'I thought I might, since I have had a go at being a knight last time.'

This did not stop her playing at sword fighting. She was really amazing at swordsmanship, even with a plastic sword. She was so quick on her feet and seemed to anticipate her opponent's every move.

Thomas and Steve took turns to fight Maya. They were good themselves. Perhaps training with Harry had given them some skills they would not otherwise have had.

Someone was watching the children sword fight. It was the Duke of Northumberland. Clearly impressed by their enthusiasm and skill, he said that he would 'dub' them knights. Maya, if that were what she wished, would be Lady Maya. Thomas's mum and dad were thrilled and took photos of the ceremony. The 'knighting' was just for fun and it was something that happened occasionally at the Knights' Yard.

'Arise, Sir Thomas Malton,' said the duke, gently touching Thomas's shoulder with his sword, as Thomas knelt before him.

'Thank you, your d...' Thomas was about to say 'dukiness', but looking up he saw Dad, Steven and Maya laughing at him, 'Your Grace'. He saw someone else smiling at him. It was Harry!

Thomas nudged Maya and Steve, who turned to look at Harry.

Thomas saw that the duke was looking in that direction too. Had the duke seen Harry? Thomas had a feeling he had. The duke turned to talk to Thomas' mum and dad and steered them towards the trebuchet activity game.

This allowed Steve, Thomas and Maya to greet Harry. Harry bowed to Lady Maya, then presented her with a beautiful amber necklace and praised her bravery. Maya smiled and said, 'Thank you.' Harry had presents for Thomas and Steve too. These were spurs. 'You've won your spurs and achieved your quest, Sir Thomas and Sir Steve. What was it Lady Maya said, Sir Thomas? "Keep its ee frae the baal?" You threw the baal in its ee!' They all laughed.

Thomas could see that the duke was glancing towards them. His parents were about to rejoin the friends. Harry had noticed this too, and said farewell. He walked over to his horse, mounted and rode out of the yard, turning to wave as he left. No one in the yard, other than the three friends (and quite possibly the duke) seemed to know he was there.

Thomas, Maya and Steve ran to the door of the yard. They watched as Harry rode past his statue, spurred his horse into a gallop, and then disappeared, exactly as he had the day Thomas had first seen him.

Harry

The Lambton Worm

by C.M. Leumane

*One Sunday morn young Lambton
went a-fishin' in the Wear;
An' catched a fish upon his heuk,
He thowt leuk't varry queer,
But whatt'n a kind of fish it was
Young Lambton couldn't tell.
He waddn't fash to carry it hyem,
So he hoyed it in a well.*

Chorus:

*Whisht! lads, haad yor gobs,
Aa'll tell ye aall an aaful story,
Whisht! lads, haad yor gobs,
An' Aall tell ye 'boot the worm.*

*Noo Lambton felt inclined to gan
An' fight in foreign wars.
He joined a troop o' Knights that cared
for neither wounds nor scars,
An' off he went to Palestine
Where queer things him befel,
An' varry seun forgot aboot
The queer worm i' the well.*

*Whisht! lads, haad yor gobs,
Aa'll tell ye aall an aaful story,
Whisht! lads, haad yor gobs,
An' Aall tell ye 'boot the worm.*

But the worm got fat an' growed an' growed,
An' growed an aaful size;
He'd greet big teeth, a greet big gob,
An' greet big goggle eyes.
An' when at neets he craaled aboot
To pick up bits o'news,
If he felt dry upon the road,
He milked a dozen coos.

> *Whisht! lads, haad yor gobs,*
> *Aa'll tell ye aall an aaful story,*
> *Whisht! lads, haad yor gobs,*
> *An' Aall tell ye 'boot the worm.*

This fearful worm wad often feed
On calves an' lambs an' sheep,
An' swally little bairns alive
When they laid doon to sleep.
An' when he'd eaten aall he cud
An' he had had he's fill,
He craaled away an' lapped his tail
Seven times roond Pensher Hill.

> *Whisht! lads, haad yor gobs,*
> *Aa'll tell ye aall an aaful story,*
> *Whisht! lads, haad yor gobs,*
> *An' Aall tell ye 'boot the worm.*

The news of this most aaful worm
An' his queer gannins on
Seun crossed the seas, gat to the ears
Of brave an' bowld Sir John.
So hyem he cam an' catched the beast
An' cut 'im in three halves,
An' that seun stopped he's eatin' bairns,
An' sheep an' lambs and calves.

> *Whisht! lads, haad yor gobs,*
> *Aa'll tell ye aall an aaful story,*
> *Whisht! lads, haad yor gobs,*
> *An' Aall tell ye 'boot the worm.*

So noo ye knaa hoo aall the folks
On byeth sides of the Wear
Lost lots o' sheep an' lots o' sleep
An' lived in mortal feor.
So let's hev one to brave Sir John
That kept the bairns frae harm,
Saved coos an' calves by myekin' haalves
O' the famis Lambton Worm.

> *Whisht! lads, haad yor gobs,*
> *Aa'll tell ye aall an aaful story,*
> *Whisht! lads, haad yor gobs,*
> *An' Aall tell ye 'boot the worm.*

Noo lads, Aa'll haad me gob,
That's aall Aa knaa aboot the story
Of Sir John's clivvor job
Wi' the aaful Lambton Worm.

Witness 2000 years of Northumbrian history and success

in

A PORTRAIT of ACHIEVEMENT

NORTH EAST ENGLAND BY D.H.WILLIAMS MCIM

This fascinating book celebrates the collective achievements of many who have contributed over the last two thousand years to making the North East of England famous.

Packed with useful information and rare archive images, complemented by stunning new colour photographs from the author, this quality publication is a testament to all those who, from Roman times to the present day, have made their mark through commerce, industry, sport, entertainment and the arts, and is written for anyone with an interest in, or merely a curiosity about the achievements of the region.

Hardback • 270 pages • 303 x 215mm
Available from selected independent retailers or direct from the publisher **AC Group** priced **£29.95**

For further details about this, other publications, art and collectables visit **www.kingdomofnorthumbria.co.uk**

KQ06